"Why do you want to kiss me? And why does it scare you?" Heather asked.

Rob smiled into her eyes, feeling shivers of fear and excitement racing through her. "You know the answer to both questions. And you're just as scared."

"God, yes," she breathed, and he felt her hot breath against his lips.

"We're connected, Heather, in ways we don't even know yet. But we'll learn. Together."

"No." She shook her head and her hair whispered across his wrist.

He turned his head and captured a fistful of its silk. "I know what you want." He pressed his lips to the wild pulse at her throat. "I can feel it. . . ."

WHAT ARE *LOVESWEPT* ROMANCES?

They are stories of true romance and touching emotion. We believe those two very important ingredients are constants in our highly sensual and very believable stories in the *LOVESWEPT* line. Our goal is to give you, the reader, stories of consistently high quality that may sometimes make you laugh, sometimes make you cry, but are always fresh and creative and contain many delightful surprises within their pages.

Most romance fans read an enormous number of books. Those they truly love, they keep. Others may be traded with friends and soon forgotten. We hope that each *LOVESWEPT* romance will be a treasure—a "keeper." We will always try to publish

LOVE STORIES YOU'LL NEVER FORGET
BY AUTHORS YOU'LL ALWAYS REMEMBER

The Editors

Loveswept ® 605

Judy Gill
Healing Touch

BANTAM BOOKS

NEW YORK · TORONTO · LONDON · SYDNEY · AUCKLAND

HEALING TOUCH

A Bantam Book / March 1993

If you would be interested in receiving protective vinyl
covers for your Loveswept books, please write to this address
for information:

Loveswept
Bantam Books
P.O. Box 985
Hicksville, NY 11802

ISBN 0-553-44372-0

Published simultaneously in the United States and Canada

PRINTED IN THE UNITED STATES OF AMERICA

OPM   0 9 8 7 6 5 4 3 2 1

One

Heather Tomasi! What the hell was she doing in his head again?

In the hours since his niece, April's, latest storm of tears and temper, Major Rob McGee, newly appointed base surgeon at Canadian Forces Base, Comox, single foster parent and onetime playboy, had come to a startling realization about his life. That had got him thinking about Heather, though why she should come to mind the minute he decided he needed a wife was beyond his comprehension. Heather Tomasi was no more wife material than he was husband material.

He intended to become husband material, though, and fast, because April needed a permanent mother figure in her life. And maybe, just maybe, it was time he had a wife anyway.

The biggest problem was, he thought, sitting on the back step and digging his toe into a crack in the sidewalk, he was the proverbial new kid in town.

Where was he going to find a woman? Once, that wouldn't have fazed him at all. But he'd hardly dated at all since his niece had come to live with him. He was two years out of practice. His social life had come to a grinding halt when April's maternal grandmother—who'd been the girl's guardian since the death of her parents—had remarried. The lady had discovered that raising a little girl was not conducive to the kind of lifestyle she and her new husband wanted, so bingo! Rob McGee became a surrogate daddy overnight.

Not only that, but Comox was a small military base in a small town, and a guy couldn't just stop some likely looking woman on the street and say, "Hi. Let's start dating. Maybe in a month or two we can start talking about marriage. Do you like kids?"

There had to be an easier way than that to locate a potential mate. But, like what? Like asking to get fixed up? "Hah!"

The sound of his own derisive bark startled him. He scowled. Well, why not? he asked himself. There had to be a first time for everything, and this was the first time he'd ever seriously contemplated marriage. Furthermore, he didn't know anybody for a radius of several hundred miles besides his longtime good pal, Eric Lind, and Eric's zany wife, Sylvia.

And Heather Tomasi.

Rob felt something inside him lurch as her name popped into his head again. Dammit, he wished she'd go away and leave him alone with his misery, but she wouldn't. Against his will, his mind saw Heather Tomasi, whom he had met once, two years ago, stationing herself against the sagging backyard fence.

Her image smiled. He grimaced. A woman like Heather Tomasi did not belong in Permanent Married Quarters, not even in his imagination. She was the kind of woman he'd dated before April had come to live with him. She was not the kind of woman he should be thinking of now. He needed a wifely kind of woman. A motherly kind. Not one who got her kicks out of living too close to the edge.

What he needed was a domestic kind of woman. Like Sylvia. Though looking at her, who'd have guessed it? According to Eric, she'd always made her way through the world with a cocky insouciance that had bedeviled him when they'd first met. Who would have thought she'd be so willing to give up her personal courier business and a life of flitting from one airport to another to marry an air force pilot and raise babies wherever he might happen to get posted?

Of course, Rob thought, maybe she made such a great wife and mother because she'd always been good with kids. So good, after all, that April's grandmother had chosen her to bring April to him in Germany. He'd managed to break his leg skiing in the Dolomites the day before April arrived, and Sylvia refused to leave April alone with Eric, which led to Sylvia and Eric falling in love.

Now, two years and one set of twins later, Eric and Sylvia were still so obviously nutty about each other, it sometimes got downright embarrassing to watch them. But they had acquired a large circle of friends since they'd come to Comox a year or so earlier, especially since Eric had started giving private flying lessons.

Maybe they could help him find someone.

Rob shook his head. In that direction lay total humiliation. He had his reputation to think of. And Eric had a flatteringly exaggerated belief in Rob's abilities to *cherchez les femmes*. He sighed, smashed a mosquito on his neck, watched a few lights go out in nearby houses, and thought about couples retiring for the night together in blissful matrimony. Heaving himself to his feet, he went inside.

Sighing again, he picked up the phone and punched in the one familiar number he could reach without dialing long distance. "Hi, Sylvia. It's Rob. I hope it's not too late to call. Could I speak to Eric, please?"

Five minutes later he hung up, not sure which emotion to go with, total embarrassment at having had to ask to get fixed up or elation that Eric and Sylvia had already been planning a barbecue on his and April's behalf, to welcome them and introduce them to their friends.

They were good people to know, Eric and Sylvia Lind. Really good people. And surely even a woman like Sylvia had lots of domestically inclined friends.

"Heather. Spare me a minute, will you?"

Hearing the familiar voice, Heather Tomasi paused in her dash toward the weight room of the health club she owned with three others. She turned and smiled at her sweat-soaked friend, Sylvia Lind, who was a frequent customer. Sylvia despaired of ever losing the "blubber" on her tummy, put there by carrying twins, and worked out three times weekly. Personally, Heather thought Sylvia's one-year-old twins were worth every bit of extra flesh her friend might be carrying around—not that there was much.

Heather took her headband off and shook her hair loose. "Walk along with me, Sylvia. I have to see El for a minute before I head out to the canyon." Ellie Grayson, her assistant, saw her beckoning wave and waited for her at the door to the weight room.

"How are my favorite babies?" Heather asked Sylvia.

Sylvia shoved her light brown hair back. "Crabby. I'd sell them both for a dime." Despite her words, her golden eyes glowed with love. "Shanna has a new tooth just showing and Shane will cut his by tomorrow, which will make them much happier children on Saturday. Which brings me to the subject. Can you come for a barbecue then?"

Heather smiled. She seldom passed up a chance to play with Sylvia's babies. "Love to. What can I bring?"

"Your sexy presence will be enough." Sylvia gave her a sidelong glance. "You still in the market for a pseudo boyfriend to keep your folks off your case next month?"

Heather shrugged. "Not really. My grandmother's right, you know. I am a grown-up. I should be able to face up to my parents' disappointment in me. And they're adults, too, and should be able to accept me the way I am."

Sylvia frowned faintly. "Well, it's up to you, of course, but you're the one who asked me last month if I knew anybody who'd do. I've thought of someone, and if you're interested, he'll be at the barbecue Saturday. He's a medical officer. Think how that would please your dad. And the uniform! Your mother would take one look at the gold braid and epaulets, see establishment and pure conservatism, and swoon with joy."

"Well, you're right on both counts, but . . ."

"Think about it," Sylvia said as she pressed her splayed hand to the door of the women's shower room. "By the way, you have met him. Eric's best man at our wedding. Rob McGee, uncle of the little girl I escorted to Germany when I met Eric." She stepped inside the shower room. "Remember?"

The door swung shut in Heather's face. She stared at it, her heart tilting dangerously in her chest. Did she remember Rob McGee? Oh boy, did she remember! Talk about gold braid and epaulets! But "establishment?" Rob McGee didn't know the meaning of the word.

His naughty green eyes had reflected the color of his uniform as they'd raked over her with a boldness that had taken her breath away. They'd made secret promises that had left her knees weak and set up the kind of silly, fluttery response in her that she knew better than to trust. Even while she'd been reeling from the sensations he elicited from twenty feet away, a secret part of her had itched to get closer and see what would happen if they touched.

She'd found out when they danced, and to be honest, it had scared the living daylights out of her. The sensations he aroused in her had reminded her of those first, incredible times with Gerald, and then she had felt sick to her stomach.

But he wasn't Gerald, she'd told herself. She was fifteen years older than when she'd first met Gerald, and better able to control those feelings. Maybe, she'd thought with dizzying hope, she was finally healed. Yet, even while part of her had longed for a chance to get to know Rob better, her more sensible self had been grateful that he was leaving almost at once, returning to his base thousands of miles away in Germany.

And now he was back.

Shaking off a shivery sensation, she spoke briefly to her assistant, then jogged out to the parking lot. She would put Rob McGee right out of her mind.

At least until Saturday afternoon, and the barbecue.

"Thanks," Rob said, accepting the beer Eric handed him. He popped the tab as he looked around at the swirling collection of adults and children. April, to his pleased amazement, had left his side within moments of their arrival, lured away by a couple of little girls "to see the puppies." And she thought she couldn't make friends!

Of the women, dressed in everything from denim to silk, some were obviously attached, and those who weren't didn't look particularly domestic to him. But what did he know? He'd never looked at a woman before as a potential spouse.

He glanced out the window to see smoke rising from somewhere in the yard below the deck. There'd be food on the barbecue. Maybe the single but domestic women were down there, aproned and oven mitted, cooking or arranging salads and pies, or whatever it was domestically inclined females did. He could only hope.

A slinky brunette sidled by, giving him a long look from under her lashes. She had tattoos all over both bare arms and up her legs as far as he could see, which was really, really far.

He frowned at Eric. "I'm not sure this was such a good idea."

"Don't worry. It was a fine idea," Eric assured him, opening a can of ginger ale. "There's this one friend of Sylvia's we both think is going to be just right for you." He grinned, and something about that grin bothered Rob.

"She may not realize it right off the bat," Eric went on, "but believe me, she's one ripe and ready female, and she's in love with our babies. All you have to do is convince her that she'd like to raise some of her own. Plus April, of course."

Rob stared, beer can halfway to his lips. "Now, hold on. I don't want to have to take the trouble to 'convince' any woman. I want one who's going to be as eager as I am to make a home for April. One who's willing and interested and ready to make a commitment to marriage. And motherhood."

"Since when has it been 'trouble' for you to persuade a lady to see things your way? Don't you hold the World's Cup in seduction? I'm counting on you to clip this one's wings before she reminds Sylvia how much fun it is to be single. She's due for her comeuppance." Eric laughed. "Overdue. And she's exactly your type."

Rob snorted in exasperation. "Get real! This just shows you don't know me anymore. My life's changed since I got April. I'm not looking for someone you think is my type. I'm looking for someone to turn into a *wife*."

Eric gazed at him with all the wisdom of a man married for two years, and with pity for an individual less blessed. "My son, you wouldn't be happy with a wife who wasn't your type."

Rob stared at his beer can. He wasn't sure he'd be happy with any kind of wife at all, but his happiness wasn't the only consideration. Of course, he would give marital bliss a damn good try if he found the right woman. He looked up and met Eric's gaze, surprised and a bit chagrined to see compassion and understanding in Eric's eyes.

They'd been good friends for more than ten years, and had shared a house in Germany for three of those. Maybe it was time to trust Eric's judgment. Nobody, when it came right down to it, knew him better.

So, all right. He'd asked Eric for help. The least he could do was see what his friend had produced.

He shrugged and grinned. "Okay, jet jock, I suppose we'd better get moving. Bring on the dames."

Rob came to an abrupt halt, slopping beer out of the can. It ran down his hand as he stared at her. He recognized her. He also recognized the tightening of his gut as his body responded to the sight of her.

There they were again, all those memories he'd tried to put away permanently: the lilt of her voice, the cadence of her laughter, the sensation of her breath soft against his skin, and the lightness of her in his arms when they danced. He could almost feel again the beat of the music, how it had pulsed through the air and into his bones.

He recalled with sharp clarity the way their gazes had met and clung for breathtakingly long moments, the way the two of them had communicated silently. He had asked without words, What if? And her eyes had replied, Who knows? They both had known that if he hadn't had to rush away from the wedding reception to get back to Germany and April, the question, and the answer, would have been different.

Two years. Two years and his body still remembered what he had successfully put out of his mind until recently.

He dug in his heels. "Eric, are you off your stick? That's not wife material, that's—"

But Eric wasn't listening. He was heading straight for his wife, who was standing beside Heather Tomasi. He ran a hand through Sylvia's hair, and drew her head onto his shoulder, looking as if they'd been apart for days, not minutes.

Heather watched as Sylvia slipped an arm around her husband's back, then looked away as the two kissed. She felt like a voyeur, and felt an odd kind of envy, too, though marriage was the last thing on her agenda.

As she swung her gaze away it collided with Rob McGee's, and everything went still inside her.

Rob felt the impact of that collision and got lost in the depths of Heather Tomasi's big, shining eyes, so deep a brown, they were almost black. She clearly was not surprised to see him. She smiled, and just like the first time he'd seen her, he felt like he'd been turned inside out.

Sylvia and Eric broke their kiss. Sylvia smiled at Rob, then turned to her friend. "Heather, you remember Rob McGee, don't you? Rob, Heather Tomasi. You met at our wedding."

"I remember," Rob said, getting a grip on himself. "Hello, Heather. It's nice to see you again." Nice? *Nice?*

She wore red, the color she'd worn at the wedding. This time it was a flame-colored sundress with big white polka dots. Her hair, shiny black, was pulled away from her face, then allowed to fall over her shoulders and down her back in cascades of long corkscrew ringlets. A white belt encircled her narrow waist. White sandals showcased slender feet and ankles. Her skin was honey-gold with an early-summer tan.

She set her drink on the deck railing and extended her hand. He took it. Hers was cool from the ice in her glass, smooth skinned, and fine boned. Her grip was firm.

"Hello, Rob," she said, smiling. "I understand you've just been stationed here. Are you happy to be home again? Or is Comox so far from your home that it feels like another foreign posting?"

So she remembered that he was from the Maritime Provinces on the eastern end of Canada. Just as he remembered that she didn't live there on Vancouver Island, but on the mainland. Which was a mercy. "Anywhere I throw my duffle bag is home," he said, gazing directly into her glittering eyes. There was a hint of excitement in them, a touch of promise, and a bubbling, secret amusement that beckoned to him, daring him to share with her the wonderful joke that they both knew life to be.

Only . . . the joke life had played on him was that while he might want a woman like Heather Tomasi, what he needed was a woman completely unlike her.

Belatedly, he let go of her hand. "Are you visiting for the weekend?" *Please say that you don't live next door or something,* part of him pleaded, but another part of him rejoiced when she shook her head.

"Shortly after these two got married, I moved to Miracle Beach, twenty miles or so north of here, to live near my grandparents." She grinned. "Eric still believes that I had some mystical influence on the military authorities and got his squadron moved out of Cold Lake, Alberta, just so I could play with Shanna and Shane. Don't you?" she added, turning to smile at their hosts.

She looked blankly back at Rob. "Oh! Where did they go?"

Rob didn't care. "I don't know." As he gazed into her eyes again he tightened his grip on his beer can and took a large gulp of beer to wet his dry throat.

"Oh well, they've done their duty by us." Heather shrugged one slim, bare shoulder. He watched her hair slide over it. Oh, Lord! Her hair. He remembered how it had smelled, how it had felt. He remembered the silk of her skin, the strength of the toned muscles in her back. Dancing with Heather Tomasi had been a totally sensual experience. And he was a sensual man.

"Sylvia always throws great parties," Heather went on, "and then enjoys them as much as anyone else." She hitched herself up onto the railing, crossing her legs at the ankles, and swinging them idly. Picking up her glass, she tilted her head back as she drained it.

He stepped in close and slid an arm behind her lest she lean back too far. "Heights don't bother you, do they?" he asked, glancing at the ground fifteen feet below.

She looked over her shoulder, as if only then becoming aware of where she sat. "No. Not at all."

The breeze fluttered the hem of her dress, pushing it up her thighs. Casually, she smoothed it back onto her knees. She wore no stockings. If he'd been the kind of man who prayed for small favors, he'd have sent up one for a stiffer breeze.

"Do they bother you?" she asked.

Her legs? "Bother me?"

"Heights. Do you have a fear of them?"

He blinked. "Not . . . ordinarily."

Her smile threatened to send him into flight, if not actual orbit. That, he discovered, he did have a fear of. And a terrible fascination for. This was not what he'd come there for.

"Good," she said, and her approval made him feel the way he had when he was eight and Miss Larson had stuck a gold star on the back of his hand for having cleaned off the blackboards perfectly.

He leaned on the rail, feeling the warmth of her back against his arm, the warmth of her smile on his soul. "Why 'good?'" he asked.

Her eyes flirted with him. "Because I have a plan, a treat to welcome you home."

A treat? And it involved great heights? What was she going to do, fall into his arms and make love to him, carrying him aloft with passion? He swallowed another mouthful of beer, struggling with the knowledge that a man who was the sole caretaker of a child didn't take unnecessary risks with life and limb and sanity, regardless of what the treats, or rewards, might be. A man who was the sole caretaker of a young girl puts her needs first.

The fantasies persisted, though, of him climbing a steep mountainside with Heather Tomasi, reaching the summit and finding only sky above, a world spread far below, and Heather . . . Or maybe it would be something like skydiving. Floating through the air, arms outspread, their hands linked, her face upturned to his, her eyes filled with the rapture of . . .

"Look, Uncle Robbie!" April's voice dragged him back to reality.

She tore up the back steps, carrying a fat, furry puppy and wearing a bigger smile than he'd seen in ages. Her blouse had come untucked from her skirt and one sock hung down in a grubby rumple. That, however, was typical.

She leaned against him, her face shining with unaccustomed exhilaration. He had to smile back at her. It was good, seeing her look so happy.

"Heather, this is my niece, April," he said, giving the girl a quick hug. "April, Ms. Tomasi."

Heather leaned forward to shake hands with the child. "Hi, April. I've heard lots about you. Sylvia's very happy that you and your uncle have come to live so close. Who's this you have here?"

"She hasn't got a name yet." April cuddled the russet-colored pup under her chin for a moment before thrusting the warm, wiggly bundle into Rob's hands. "Isn't she sweet, Uncle Robbie?" Her eyes pleaded with him and he stroked the puppy. He knew how much she wanted one, but knew just as well how impossible it was for him to get her one at present.

When he was silent, April did something she rarely did. She asked for something. "May I have her? Please, Uncle Robbie? Sylvia said it's okay." She paused, looked apologetic, then added almost in a whisper, "And I really do miss Ajax. You said you'd see about getting us a dog when we're settled."

He hated to deny her this. "April, honey, we're not what you'd call settled," he said, handing the dog back to her. "We aren't even completely unpacked."

Her face closed up. She bent and set the pup down while she pulled up her sock. "Okay. I know. But as soon as you find yourself a wi—"

He dropped his beer.

It splashed over April's feet, and the little dog immediately began to lap up the foam that oozed across the deck. April grabbed the pup and held it away from the beer as Rob tried to wipe it up with a handful of paper napkins. "That's bad for babies," she admonished the dog. She turned to Heather, and asked, "Have you seen Sylvia's babies, Miss To-masi?"

"Call me Heather, and yes I have." She grinned. "They're even cuter than puppies. Maybe you should ask Uncle Robbie for a couple of them, instead."

Rob choked as he abruptly straightened. Before he could say a word, April sighed heavily and said, "He hasn't even got a wife. Babies need mothers, you know."

Heather's expression turned grave as she nodded. "Yes. I do know."

"And puppies," Rob said, determined to change the subject at all costs, "need someone at home with them during the day. So until we find a housekeeper, April, the puppy will have to wait." To end the discussion, he pointed out into the yard where Magda, Eric and Sylvia's Irish setter, was striding back and forth in agitation. "I think there's a mother out there who's getting anxious about one of her babies. Take the puppy back to her, please, honey."

"Yes, Uncle Rob."

"She's a pretty little girl," Heather said as April scampered away. "I understand she went to a German school while you lived there. How's she adapting to our ways?"

Rob grimaced. "Not too well. She hates her new school, hasn't made any friends, and spends her time at home either moping in her room or flying into a rage."

He gazed after April, shaking his head ruefully. "Where do you see 'pretty?' Her hair never lies down, her ears are too big, her legs are too long and gangly, and she seems to pick up grime right out of the air. And nothing ever stays tucked in on her. I love her dearly, but she's a mess."

"Don't worry," Heather said. "She'll straighten out. All little girls go through the ugly-duckling stage."

He looked from April to Heather and smiled. "Even you?"

"Even me."

He chuckled. "It's hard to believe you were ever at the awkward age." His gaze traveled over her, from her gently swinging feet, up her shapely legs to her slender body, across her lovely face to her jet black curls, which were being lightly tousled by the breeze. Unable to restrain himself, he reached out and wrapped one of those curls around a finger, smoothing it with his thumb then letting it go. It bounced back into a long spiral that danced against the side of her neck. He looked into her eyes. "You're a swan now, Ms. Tomasi."

She smiled slowly. "Thank you, Major McGee."

He knew he should walk away. He knew the dangers of getting embroiled with a woman like her when he'd already made up his mind that he needed an entirely different kind of woman. Still, nothing could have held back his words: "Are you busy tomorrow?"

She nodded. "As a matter of fact, I am, but—"

"If not tomorrow, then another day soon." He swallowed, feeling unexpectedly callow. "I'd really like to see you again."

She met his gaze unwaveringly, a delighted smile dancing over her features like sunshine on the sea. "Well, good. That makes things easier, doesn't it?"

He blinked. Good Lord! Had Eric come right out and announced to her what Rob's intentions were? Announced to the likes of Heather Tomasi that he was looking for a wife? And she was sitting there, not running away? Something that might have been hope flickered within him. Could she possibly be domestic in disguise? If so, it was some disguise!

"How does it make things easier?" he asked.

Her smile was nothing short of enigmatic. "Let's not worry about that just yet," she said, and there was that half-hidden excitement in her eyes again. "First, let's talk about tomorrow. I'm busy, but you're welcome to join me." She looked him up and down. "In fact, I have a wild suggestion with your name on it. The treat I mentioned earlier."

The sides of his beer can dented in. "Treat?"

Her head tilted to one side as she ran her gaze over him again, as if assessing his strength and abilities. Part of him became very strong, and he definitely wanted to show her his abilities. "Have you ever bungeed?" she asked.

That wasn't what he had in mind! "Bungee *jumped*?" He stared at her. "No."

She looked sympathetic. "I guess maybe it hasn't

caught on in Europe yet. Well, now's your opportunity."

He glanced across the yard at April, still cuddling a puppy as she sat on the grass beside the mother dog. "I don't think so, thanks."

"Why not?" She laughed lightly, almost mockingly, and his normally solid ego quivered as if it had been kicked. "It's a real thrill."

"Thrill?" he echoed. "Why would any sane person want to jump off a tower with elastics around his legs and bounce around upside down?"

She arched her black eyebrows. "Goodness! Can this be the notorious Uncle Robbie asking? What about the legendary derring-do? Where is the man who told me how much he enjoyed ballooning in the Alps, taking chances on updrafts and downdrafts and perilous mountain crags? The man who spelunked his way through the deepest caverns of Spain and France? The man who reportedly spends all his leisure time in search of new adventures?"

He almost hated to admit it to her, but he had to. So much for his wanting to see her again. So much for his fantasies. Now she'd hop off the railing and go in search of a more daring man.

"Everything I ever did, I did right side up," he said. "And the derring-do, the adventure seeking, are far in the past." He heaved an exaggerated sigh. "I'm a changed man, Ms. Tomasi."

She frowned as she swept her gaze over him again. "Maybe," she said, but doubtfully, then she smiled again. It was obvious she didn't believe him. "But I'm sure you'll find the adventurousness tucked away in the bottom of your duffle bag when you unpack.

Anyway, bungee jumping is merely fun, not dangerous. And it is a great adventure."

Regretfully, he shook his head.

"Come on, Major. I don't need you to act conservative until next month."

He blinked. "Act conservative?"

Her teeth, very white and very even, pinched her
lower lip for a second. She looked momentarily
uneasy.

"What happens next month?" he asked.

"Nothing I intend to worry about now. Are you sure
you won't change your mind and come jumping with
me?"

"Heather . . ." Oh Lord, it would be something, he
thought, exploring life, looking for adventures with
this very tempting woman. He got lost in the depths
of her eyes again and sighed silently.

As if she could read his thoughts, she smiled and
said huskily, "Am I tempting you?"

He slid his hand up her back to her shoulder,
under her hair, releasing a tantalizing trace of her
perfume. "Very much." The hoarseness of his voice
surprised him. His attempt at a relaxed smile didn't,
he was sure, quite make it.

"I mean," she said, flirting with her incredibly long
eyelashes, "tempting you to try bungee jumping."
Flutter, flutter. "Tomorrow morning." Flicker, flicker.
"At seven." She hopped off the railing and darted
another glance at him through her lashes. Smiling,
she bent toward him, affording him another whiff of
her perfume, and whispered, "Naked."

He squeezed his eyes shut. His breath escaped too
swiftly, leaving him feeling deprived of oxygen. Lord
love a duck! *Naked* bungee jumping? What next?

.

He forced his eyes open, and when he looked, she was walking away from him, her body swaying in time to the rock music pulsing up out of the basement as she danced down the steps to the backyard, the hem of her red dress swinging.

A moment later, as if he were attached to her by a bungee cord, he followed. But like Eric and Sylvia, she had disappeared.

Two

"Did he agree?" Sylvia asked, grinning as she grabbed Heather's arm and tugged her into the rec room. She quickly slammed the door shut before, she said, the neighbors called the law with complaints about noise. The rec room was large and bare with uncovered joists, but none of the people dancing on the concrete floor seemed to mind the lack of finishing touches. The rock music echoed nicely in the cavernous space.

Heather waited to catch her breath before answering Sylvia. It had taken a lot of willpower and effort to drag herself away from Rob McGee the way she had. She would have dearly loved to see what his response would have been. His initial reaction had been totally gratifying. He was definitely intrigued.

"I don't know if he's going to agree or not." She spoke loudly to be heard over the music. "I haven't asked him yet."

Sylvia stared at her. "Why not?"

"I'm leading up to it in my own way."

Sylvia was stern. "In other words, you're playing games! Dammit, didn't you promise me that you'd be up-front about what you wanted?"

Heather gaped at her friend. "With the playboy doctor? All I'm doing is piquing his interest. He'd never take a woman seriously! If I want him to help me, I've got to at least offer him some adventure first."

"How do you know that? Maybe he's changed. I'm warning you, Heather. You be truthful with that man every step of the way, or I'll blow the whistle on you." She paused dramatically. "To your parents."

With a peal of disbelieving laughter, Heather let herself be caught around the waist and drawn into the dancing crowd. She glanced at her partner.

Oh. Alvin. Well, why not? She was still fond of him, even though she'd broken up with him. Alvin was just so . . . intense. She waved at Sylvia, who waved back before darting up the stairs to the main floor.

Glancing up at her ex-boyfriend, Heather had a more than sneaking hunch that Sylvia had invited Alvin simply for comparison's sake. Of course, there was no comparison between him and Rob. She didn't need Sylvia to point that out.

Rob circumnavigated the backyard, stopping when he reached April to spend a few minutes with her—although she was uncharacteristically loath to take time away from her newfound friends and Sylvia's trampoline to waste it on him—then he continued his search for the tantalizing Heather. Not finding her outdoors, he returned to the sun deck and entered the kitchen, grabbing a beer on his way. Before he could open it, Sylvia walked in.

"Have you seen Heather?" he asked.

"She's downstairs. The last time I saw her she was dancing with her ex-boyfriend." She patted his cheek. "Go intervene, will you? They're both nice people, but lousy together."

Shoving his beer into her hand, he snatched open the door with more alacrity than he liked in himself. He was not going to chase after Heather Tomasi! But . . . Lousy together how? As in lousy together in bed? Oh hell, how would Sylvia know that? Heather didn't strike him as the kind of woman who would kiss and tell. Or were they simply bad for each other? Was the guy cruel to her? Rob slipped on a stair in his rush, and immediately slowed to a more casual pace.

Heather Tomasi could look after herself.

Standing halfway down the stairs, he scanned the crowd, telling himself he wasn't searching for that tumbled mass of black curls. Nevertheless, he found it immediately.

Her hair had come undone from its clip. It bounced and frothed around her glowing face as she smiled up at her partner, a mostly bald man with a ponytail, who was dressed in what appeared to be some kind of priestly vestment. Rob felt his hackles rise.

He took the rest of the stairs at a lope and twisted like a bullfighter when he reached the bottom to avoid a busty blonde with a wineglass in each hand. She gave him a quick once-over as if she might offer him one of the drinks, but he smiled at her, the kind of smile he'd long used to tell a woman that he admired her for what she was, but at the moment, regrettably, duty called.

Duty. That brought him to a halt at the edge of the dancers.

Duty did call. His duty to April, her need for stability was his loving responsibility to fulfill.

Try as he might to convince himself otherwise, he knew it sure as blazes wasn't duty that had him following Heather Tomasi. Yet even as he began to turn back, she appeared not two feet away, still dancing. Attractive as hell and tempting as sin, and absolutely not what he needed in his life.

Not what he needed in a wife.

Over her partner's shoulder, their eyes met. She smiled. The effects of that smile crept up on him unawares, then slammed into his gut, knocking him off balance. Oh, hell! How could he resist what those eyes hinted at? Just one last fling before he settled down . . . ? Wasn't a man entitled?

Deftly, he slid an arm between the roughly woven gown of the ponytailed man and Heather's slim waist. There was precious little room. That, too, did things to his hackles.

"Excuse me," he said, giving the guy a cold, toothy grin that he knew any man on earth would understand. *Let go or prepare to die.* "My dance." The man let go.

Swinging Heather away, Rob linked his hands behind her back and, with steps that approximated dancing, walked her backward toward a door on the far side of the room. As they danced, she put her hands on his shoulders, tossed her hair back, and smiled at him again. Her dark eyes gleamed with laughter.

"Where are we going?" she asked.

"I want to talk to you!" She cocked her head, but he didn't answer her silent question. He merely steered her through the door he'd spotted and into the room behind it. He shut the door and leaned on it before releasing her.

"All right, why?" he demanded.

Heather laughed, feeling wild and crazy and glad he'd followed her, glad he'd snatched her away from Alvin, glad his eyes appreciated her so openly. Lord, but the man had a knack for making her feel good. Too good. She had to be careful. She'd decided to pull off her annual charade just one more year, because she knew how favorably Rob would impress her parents. The trick was going to be in not getting too involved herself. She wanted her mother to love him. She didn't want to love him herself.

"I'm the one who should be asking why," she said. "Such as why are we having this tryst in the powder room?"

"Pow—" She saw him blink and look around the small room in momentary consternation. Then, laughing softly, he shrugged it off. Grasping her around the waist, he lifted her and sat her on the counter beside a pink marble sink. His biceps bulged under her hands as she instinctively clutched them. They were hard and they rippled, and she wanted to hold them longer. She even suffered a momentary but nearly uncontrollable urge to slide the sleeve of his blue T-shirt higher and press her cheek to one of them. Luckily, he moved away, reaching out to twist the lock on the door. Planting the toe of one white sneaker on the lid of the toilet, he leaned his folded arms on his upraised knee and grinned at her from under his thick dark blond eyebrows.

She wanted to trace those eyebrows, smooth them down, then run her fingers into his blond hair and ruffle it. Oh, heaven help her, it was happening again. With him she was in danger of forgetting what she knew to be true about herself. She wouldn't just have to be careful. She'd have to be super cautious. Either that, or decide against him entirely.

"As I said," he began, "I want to talk to you and we can at least hear each other in here." He paused. "And we won't be interrupted."

"No?" she said, as somebody knocked on the door. She crossed her legs, spreading the full skirt of her dress over her knees. "But what makes you think I want to talk to you? I was dancing."

His grin broadened, and twin creases slashed his face, bracketing his mouth. It was a firm mouth, but she was certain it could be tender. She shivered deep inside, wondering what it would feel like on her. Oh, stop!

"I'm a lot better dancer," he said, "not to mention better looking, than the dude wearing the robe and sandals. And you wanted to talk to me," he added softly, "more than you wanted to dance with him, or you'd have said no."

She raised her eyebrows. "Did you give me a chance?"

He raised his in return. "Do you wait to be 'given' your chances, Ms. Tomasi, or do you make them for yourself?"

She only smiled, wondering if he had any idea how hard her heart was racing. Probably. He was a very experienced man. And perceptive.

"Besides," he continued, "you issued a provocative invitation, then walked away. You intended me to follow." He tapped the tip of her nose with one finger. "And you intended to be caught."

He was marvelously sure of himself, she mused. He was bold and so confident of his own charm that no woman would ever need to pander to his ego. She liked that.

"And if I did?" she challenged.

"There's no *if* about it. And I want to know why."

She swung her left foot back and forth and watched his eyes fasten on the red of her toenail polish. His gaze slid up over her ankles, her calves, right to the hem of her dress, and she felt it like a caress. It made her burn.

Collecting herself, she looked straight at him. "Why what?"

He stood erect and stepped closer, touching her hair, sliding a hand through it, lifting it off her shoulders, then letting it drop back. Entranced by his touch, she felt shivers trickle down her arms and spine as though no one had ever caressed her hair before.

"Why did you issue such a challenging invitation and then run away?"

He asked the question in a gruff voice, as if half-angry with her. But then he touched her lower lip with his thumb and said under his breath, "God, but I want to kiss you when you look at me like that."

Her heart did a belly flop, startling her with its instability. Her lips parted as he traced the shape of her mouth. She spoke against his thumb, flesh moving on flesh. "Are you going to?"

After a beat, he took his hand away. "No." His gaze

bored into her eyes. He spoke softly, his voice just audible over the sound of music from the other room, but she still heard the deep note of regret in it. Somebody knocked again, then twisted the door-knob. For a second she turned her head that way, but didn't even attempt to slide off the counter. She knew she wouldn't have been able to stand.

Some inner compulsion drew her gaze back to his.

She thought he was going to say something more, perhaps explain, but he didn't. He only shook his head and brushed her hair back again. His breath came out in a long sigh, then his hand trailed down over her shoulder and arm. For a moment, she felt his fingers tremble as if he wanted to encircle her arm, maybe draw her against him, but then his touch was gone and he was leaning on the wall across from her, hands shoved into the pockets of his white pants. His sexy gaze continued to caress her, though, and a strong pulse of desire shafted through her like a pain.

"Why don't you answer my question instead?" he said, and she remembered belatedly what they'd been discussing.

"I issued that invitation because I thought you might enjoy the experience. I'm going to do it too."

He sucked in a harsh breath. "Nude?"

"Yes."

For a second she thought she saw outrage leap into his eyes, but then he squeezed them shut. His dark lashes had golden tips. When he opened his eyes again, they were clear, showing only mild inter-est. "Again, why?" he asked.

She shrugged. "Partly because my partners dared me to."

"Partners? I thought you were an aerobics instructor."

"I am." She tilted her chin up. "With a degree in phys ed. When I moved to Vancouver Island, I bought into an almost defunct health club. We've diversified, gone into other sporting activities that members of our club want to try, as well as the general public. Aer-Real Adventures offers bungee jumping, parasailing, and a few other things."

"Including bungee jumping in the raw."

He was really hung up on that. "Not always," she said. "Just this once, actually. It started out as a gag, but we soon realized it was exactly what we needed to get our business—if you'll forgive me—off the ground. It's a promotional thing and interest has been fantastic."

He didn't look even vaguely amused by the idea. A muscle jumped in his jaw. "It's a crazy thing. You can't be serious."

"Why not?" She squared her shoulders, feeling the cold mirror against her back. It didn't chill her so much as the ice in Rob's eyes, and for the first time since her initial hesitancy over the idea of a nude drop, doubts assailed her. She brought herself up short on that one. Dammit, what right did he have to make her start doubting herself? As her partners had said, skin was skin. Everybody had it. All over their bodies. And it would be very good for business, as the advance ticket sales had already proved.

"Really, it's quite safe, Rob. I have that assurance from my own physician and from several chiropractors. And I've completed over a hundred jumps with no ill effects. The cords don't snap the jumper to an abrupt stop. There's just a gradual stretching and then a gentle recoil. Why, last week two women in their seventies—one of them my own grandmother—took their first plunge and—"

"I've read the medical journal reports on it," he said impatiently, looking down at her along a beautifully proportioned nose, despite the bump on it that suggested it had once met with a hard fist. She wanted to rub a fingertip over it. She wanted to do something to soften his gaze again. She wanted his smile, his warmth, his . . . approval.

What? Where had that come from? Dammit, his approval was completely unimportant! She never looked for approval from anyone. Not anymore. It was a waste of time. Clearly she'd misjudged him, misread him. She frowned. "And what did your medical journals have to say about it?"

"The jury's still out. But you're young and strong and athletic, so I'm sure it won't do you a lot of damage." Again, that muscle in his jaw jumped, and this time there was no mistaking the anger in his eyes. "What I don't understand is why you have to do it in the buff."

Her frown deepened. "I don't *have* to do it. I choose to. Anything that brings in the public and gets the sport more recognition is good for business. Like the old saying goes, when you're second best you try harder, and Aer-Real Adventures is the newcomer on the scene. We have to play catch-up. We stand to make piles of money with this exercise too. We've sold over two hundred tickets at one hundred dollars apiece, so far."

He stared at her while he did the mental arithmetic. The result didn't lessen his objections, however. "There are that many people in the world willing to spend a hundred bucks to strip off their clothes and make fools of themselves in public?"

Money? she wondered. Was *that* his problem? "We're not charging the jumpers, for heaven's sake! We're charging the spectators."

"Spectators? Lord love a duck!" He sank back against the wall, arms folded across his chest. "You're going to let two hundred strange men pay to ogle you while you're nude?"

She met his disbelieving, censorious gaze. Irritation at his attitude warred with disappointment, with an inexplicable sense of hurt. She clenched her teeth, then shrugged negligently to show him he didn't matter to her. "I am. And I take it you're declining my invitation to join in the fun?"

"Yes. Military officers who value their commissions avoid cheap publicity stunts. And expensive ones."

She hid her hurt by goading him. "And adventure? I take it you've suddenly started to value your commission in ways you never used to."

He shrugged. "I told you. I've changed."

She slipped off the counter. "I'll say."

"I had to change," he said harshly. "Knowing a child is depending on him to be there for her, to stay alive and able-bodied to look after her, gives a man a slightly different outlook on life.

"April's an orphan because her father—my brother—had a totally irresponsible and cavalier attitude toward life. His life and his wife's. Like our father before him, he believed in his own invincibility. My father loved to take his boat out in any weather, and drowned during a storm, leaving behind a widow and two small children. My brother drove his sports car as though rules applied to everyone else, and died instantly in a crash. His wife was with him; she lingered in a coma for a week. My brother broke the rules and April's the one who pays the cost. I'm all she has. I take care of myself."

"Oh." Suddenly, Heather felt ashamed. Of course. He did have his niece to consider. Seen in that light, his refusal to participate was more understandable.

What wasn't though, in any light at all, was his obvious disapproval of her for doing it. Sylvia had slipped a cog or two, trying to fix her up with a man like the new and definitely not improved Major McGee.

Yet, why was she hurt? He shouldn't have any power to hurt her. How could a man gaze at her and make her feel beautiful and exciting and worthwhile, then in the next moment make her feel small and cheap and unworthy? She hated feeling that way. She'd spent too much of her life fighting to overcome such insecurities.

She wished she'd never asked him. She almost wished that she was what her parents wanted her to be, so Rob McGee would look at her again as he had before, with admiration, with pleasure, instead of with such censure.

She stood taller, squaring her shoulders, and met his stare. What was the matter with her, anyway? What made her think his opinion was of any importance? It wasn't. She was having some kind of brainstorm here, locked into this little room with him.

"I'm sorry if I've disappointed you," he said.

"It doesn't matter," she lied. "I merely thought you might get a charge out of giving our female guests a thrill, but if not . . ." She shrugged again. "Don't worry about it. There'll be plenty of other takers." She unlocked the door and swung it open, wanting only to escape. "I'm sure you'll excuse me now."

"Heather, wait." He caught her arm, turning her back into the room, oblivious to the two women who waited their turns to enter.

"You haven't answered all my questions," he said. "What about that 'conservative' thing? What about what you wanted me to do for you next month? That's when you said you'd 'need' me."

"I won't need you," she said shortly, forcing a cool smile. "It was a misuse of the term. I never 'need' any man, at any time, for anything. Haven't you heard, Major? About men and buses?" She tossed her hair back over her shoulder. "Enjoy the rest of the party."

She stepped out and, with a bow and a sweeping gesture of her arm, indicated the powder room—and Rob McGee. "Ladies, help yourselves."

Rob caught up with Heather again between the two barbecues. He wrapped his hand around her upper arm, feeling her firm, cool skin, resilient under his fingers, and the sleek muscles underneath. She flipped her hair over her shoulder and glanced up at him without expression, her eyes as cool as her skin. Yet he thought he glimpsed an underlying warmth there, too, that she couldn't hide.

He took a plate from a nearby stack and handed it to her.

"Hot dog?" he asked, turning her to the barbecue on the left. "Hamburger? Corn on the cob?"

She shook her head, still solemn.

"Sulking?"

Her eyes widened. "Not at all."

He helped himself to an ear of corn and urged her toward the other barbecue. They waited until the people ahead of them had moved on toward the salad table, then he suggested she have some salmon.

She declined, and he wondered if she had become a vegetarian. That might make things difficult. Both he and April were very fond of meat and— He broke off the thought with an impatient shake of his head. Dammit, when would he remember that Heather Tomasi was not the woman he was looking for?

Next time she walked away from him, he would not go traipsing after her like an idiot.

She gently twisted her arm, removing it from his clasp, then selected a can of iced tea from a tub of ice.

"Are we fighting?" he asked, taking a dripping beer bottle from the tub.

She cast him a sidelong glance. Was that a spark of laughter in the depths of her eyes? "Of course not. What would we have to fight about?"

"Maybe you think if you get mad at me, I'll change my mind about joining you tomorrow?"

This time, the laughter he saw in her eyes bubbled out of her mouth. "Why would I want you to change your mind? Like I said, there'll be plenty of jumpers to entertain the ticket holders."

"You did leave in a huff."

She shrugged and gave him a small smile. "Maybe. You did sound a tad like my father when he's giving me his annual lecture on the advisability of settling down. But I never stay mad long."

"Good." He held a large spoonful of potato salad over her plate, but she shook her head. While he was heaping it onto his plate along with slices of tomato and cucumber, she escaped to the dessert table.

He caught up with her quickly. "Do you intend to take your father's advice?"

Her laughter rang out, pure and sweet and utterly amused. "Me? Never! I'm having far too much fun to ever want to give it up."

He stared as she loaded her plate with three brownies thick with icing, a slice of pumpkin pie laden with whipped cream, another of apple pie, and two chocolate chip cookies as big as saucers. She topped it all off with Nanaimo bars. He counted. Four. Then, after a moment's hesitation, she added a fifth.

"Sylvia cut them too small," she said as if in explanation, though he hadn't spoken. He hadn't been able to.

He followed her across the grass to where she swirled her red skirt out around her and sat, leaning her back on a stone wall, her legs curled to one side.

He joined her, feeling the warmth of the stones through his T-shirt, feeling the warmth of her thigh, though they did not touch. At least six inches separated them. He felt what he did because he wanted to, because he knew what it would be like if it did happen. When it happened.

Trying to distract himself, he stared at her plate. "That's it? That's your dinner?"

She nodded. "That's it."

"Just desserts?"

"I like desserts, but I don't know how to bake, so

when somebody else does it, I pig out. Sara Lee and I are best buddies too."

He hoped April would stay where she was, eating hot dogs and corn on the cob with the other kids under a willow tree fifteen feet away. He did not want her to see this. "What about nutrition?"

His concern didn't concern her. "Do I look malnourished?"

He could only shake his head, his medical self appalled at what she must be doing to her blood sugar level and cholesterol count. Clearly, calories weren't a problem for her.

His male self, on the other hand, was fascinated by the obvious enjoyment with which she tackled her meal of sweet things. She sank her teeth through a brownie, chewed appreciatively, then licked the icing off her top lip. When the brownie was done, she picked up a fork and attacked the pumpkin pie. She lifted a bite of it up and paused, touching the thick wave of whipped cream with the tip of her tongue, savoring it, immersed in her enjoyment, eyes closed. He watched, immersed in enjoyment of his own.

She opened her eyes and caught him staring.

"Why don't you learn how to bake?" he asked.

"I don't have the time or the interest. I'm too busy doing other things."

He fixed his gaze on the knee of his pants, near the edge of his plate. "Like naked bungee jumping."

She broke one of the big, soft cookies in half, searching for chocolate chips, prodding one out with her thumbnail and popping it into her mouth. "Among other things."

He glanced at her. "What kind of things?"

She shrugged. "What's the point in discussing it? You'd simply disapprove of that too."

He lifted his head abruptly, startled by her calm and completely unfounded accusation. "Disapprove? Me? I never disapprove of anything. Except smoking. And drinking to excess, and then only if it's one of my patients doing it. What people do is their business." He laughed. "I may have changed, Heather, but not that much."

"You disapprove of my plans for tomorrow." She ate almost half of a Nanaimo bar in one bite. They were cut quite small.

"I do not! I've simply declined to participate."

She chewed slowly, then swallowed before saying, "You got quite . . . angry thinking about it."

He frowned. "Angry? No way! Look, I'm sorry if I gave you that impression. I just . . . wondered how it all came about. Why you're going to do it. But I wasn't angry. Why would I be?"

She met his gaze, her eyes wide and solemn. "I have no idea."

"Well—" he said, but broke off as a large, hairy man joined them, slumping down beside Heather as if quite confident of his welcome.

The newcomer squeezed her shoulders, asked, "How's my favorite ultralight lady?" and took one of her Nanaimo bars. Presumably, Rob thought, to keep her "ultra" light. She introduced him to Rob as Jackie, an old friend. As if his arrival were a signal to everyone else that she and Rob weren't having a private party, soon a large crowd had gathered. Heather invited each and every one to Sunday's nude jumping, giving explicit directions about how to find the place.

Rob tried hard not to listen. He didn't want to know where the jump was to be. He didn't need to know. He damned well wasn't going!

Sylvia joined them, carrying one of her children. The baby was smeared, hands, face, arms, and hair, with something sticky and white, to which bits of grass and other substances clung. Heather, though, didn't hesitate to reach out and take the child and cuddle him.

"Shane, you scruffy little monster you." She nuzzled his cheek. Rob wondered how she knew which baby was which. "How did you get so dirty, my angel? Has your wicked mama been neglecting you, letting you roll around on the lawn?"

"His daddy gave him a marshmallow," said his wicked mama.

Heather's eyes danced, and she glanced at Rob, sharing the joke with him. "Just one marshmallow?"

Sylvia looked complacent. "That's all it takes."

Heather's face glowed with eagerness as she stood, still holding the child. "Can I give him his bath?"

"Why do you think I brought him to you? You can bathe both of them. Eric gave Shanna a marshmallow, too, and then she hugged the dog." Sylvia cocked her head, looking down at Rob. "How about you, Uncle Robbie? Want to help Auntie Heather? Get in a bit of practical experience in case you ever need it?"

If Heather had waited for his reply, he might have agreed, but she didn't. She skipped away, the baby bouncing and giggling on her shoulder. Rob declined, but not without giving too much consideration to following Heather for a third time.

Enough was enough.

In moments Sylvia left, too, and without her and Heather's sparkling personalities to hold it together, the group separated.

Heather. She was right, of course. He did disapprove of her bungee jumping in the nude. And he had been angry. He had no right to either emotion, though. The best thing to do was stay completely away from her. She wasn't his concern. For all he cared, she could jump around naked in front of a thousand men.

Three

Cool air filled the canyon, creating ribbons of mist that spread and curled over the black water swirling through the bottom of the canyon. A hundred feet away from where Rob stood, a lacy network of steel beams formed a narrow catwalk between the sheer sandstone cliffs sliced deep by aeons of water flow. Activity began on the bridge, drawing the attention of all the gathered spectators. A gate opened on one side, leading to a narrow platform Rob hadn't noticed until a man—fully clad—stepped onto it. The man worked around the small surface, as casual and relaxed as if he were on flat ground instead of a hundred and fifty feet above a thin band of water.

Would Heather be as unconcerned at this point, Rob wondered, or was she somewhere at the end of the bridge, out of his sight, psyching herself up for an ordeal? He wished he had thought to bring binoculars, as nearly everyone else had.

"Just guys up there," said one spectator as another man, also completely dressed, came out onto the bridge. The man who had spoken passed his binoculars to his companion. "Nothin' good yet. All the ads said a girl's going first, though." He licked his thick lips and leered. "All skin."

"Sure," his friend said. "Everyone who jumps to-day goes all skin." He hauled a beer out of a cooler. "You volunteer, Jim, you get your money back. Wanna go?"

"Hell, no!" The two laughed. "I'm just here for the hooters."

Rob's fists clenched.

"Have a beer, buddy." The shorter, fatter man, the one with the blubbery lips, offered a can to Rob.

At six forty-five in the morning? "No thanks," he said, scarcely taking his eyes off the bridge. It was cool on the edge of the canyon. Was Heather cold? But would she likely be standing around naked waiting to jump? No. She'd be wrapped in a robe at least. He wondered, thinking of robes, if her priest-type ex-boyfriend was there, either about to jump, or in the ever-increasing crowd of paying spectators. Aer-Real Adventures was making a killing this morn-ing, and despite what she'd said about wanting him to give their "female guests a treat," there were precious few women present.

The air was sharp with the tang of evergreens and thick with a musky undertone from moss crushed by too many feet. Pressure built in him as he realized that each set of those feet belonged to a man who was there for the same reason as he. Accompanying each set of feet was a pair of eyes that would stare at Heather's body. Behind each pair of eyes was a male mind that would fantasize, speculate, covet. . . .

He glared sideways at the beer-swilling pair, but their gazes were fixed on the activity along the canyon. Rob watched, too, as at the far end of the bridge two men stepped aside, revealing Heather. A sweeping, rising roar of male voices echoed through the canyon.

Her black hair gleamed in the early rays of the sun. A long garment fluttered around her in the light breeze, looking as substantial as the flames it resembled in color. Rob looked at the jagged, misshapen cliffs that formed the canyon walls. He found himself holding his breath, longing for an earthquake, a typhoon, some other act of God that would put a stop to the jump.

It didn't happen. What did happen was a slow, portentous drumroll that echoed and rumbled off the cliffs, its tempo increasing with the sound. An amplified voice, excited, dramatic, said, "Ladies and gentlemen-en-en. Presenting-ing-ing . . . Aer-Real's very own . . . Heather Tomasee-ee-ee."

Hell! Rob thought. Had the jerk worked for a circus? Why didn't he just let her jump and get it over with?

The beat of the drum matched her measured steps, a slow, paced cadence as stately as a pavane as she paraded toward the center of the bridge like a human sacrifice approaching an altar.

As the cheering grew louder, echoing along with the drumroll, the atmosphere became frenzied.

Rob's mouth dried. Sweat slicked his hands. His stomach churned, and if he'd been able, he would have turned away. But some kind of horrified fascination kept him rooted where he stood. It was not anger he felt now, but cold, gut-wrenching fear. For Heather.

She reached her place. Her two male acolytes knelt as if in obeisance to fix the cords securely to her ankles, while the drum continued its blood-stirring rhythm. As the attendants stood and stepped back, leaving her standing alone, the drumming—and the cheers—hushed to a whisper.

Heather took two tiny steps, halting at the very brink of the platform. She raised her arms and let the red robe flutter to her feet where it lay, still teased by the breeze, flickering at her ankles like fire about to consume her pale flesh.

Golden sun bathed her. She stood like a gilt statue for an endless minute, her uplifted breasts clearly defined above her narrow waist, her flaring hips, her tapering thighs. The drumbeat intensified, its tempo quickening until it tumbled over itself with eager-ness, louder, sharper, a rat-a-tat-tat like chattering teeth and then, as Heather spread her arms and sailed off the catwalk, it crashed to a stop.

Total silence descended over the audience as Heather fell with incredible slowness through the opalescent early morning light.

Rob gripped the steel railing in both fists as she plunged downward, the rising sun slicing the length of the canyon and outlining her body. Heather Tomasi, upside down, long black hair streaming toward the earth, slim, graceful body attached by the ankles to a set of elastic cords, was a picture he'd never forget. Time lost credence. As she fell her velocity lessened gradually, until she appeared to be floating, sus-pended and weightless. Then she was on the re-bound before he realized she had even stopped, soaring toward the sky again. Now her hair caressed her bare shoulders as it had the day before while she danced. It swirled over her face, her breasts, and the pearly glow bathed her skin as she twisted and turned above the slack bungee cords.

Up she went, still on the rebound, her graceful ascent clearly practiced, her arms reaching out, and again, the sacrificial image came to Rob's mind.

Yet she lived with the air, one with it, of it and in it, a gleaming sculpture in flesh and blood.

A man groaned in ecstasy.

Real time began again.

As if the sound had been a signal, a coarse, raucous shout went up from the short, fat beer swiller. "Yay! Hooters!"

"I want it! I want it!" bellowed the man next to him as Heather started another descent into the canyon, still playing out the energy stored in her cords. "What a doll! That little bat can hang upside down in my belfry any day of the week. I'm signin' up for the next skinny-jumping event and you just watch me, brother, it's her skin I'll be jumping before it's all over. Ya-*hoo*!" he shouted as Heather flew upward again. "Shake them hooters, baby!"

Rob unlocked his fists from around the railing and swung the right one from knee level up, planting it squarely on the point of the dreamer's jaw. Then he turned and strode away, oblivious of the shocked silence behind him, oblivious of the outraged shout. When a beefy hand landed on his shoulder, he shook it off impatiently, adding two snarled words of harsh, unmistakable warning.

The other man left, returning to tend to his friend. Rob strode on.

He hadn't come for a fight. But he'd have loved one. He'd have welcomed it if the man had persisted, and he would have beaten the living hell out of him and any and all takers. His rage was unlike anything he'd ever known. It carried him forward as he marched from the site, buzzed in his head, boiled in his blood. He looked up only once to see that Heather had been reeled back in and stood on the catwalk again, body safely obscured by her robe.

He wanted to go and grab her down from that place, to toss her over his shoulder and carry her away, but he didn't stop marching until he'd reached his car at the bottom of the gorge. He got in, slammed the door, and stared at his split knuckles as he became aware of an ache in his bruised hand, and rested his forehead on the wheel.

"Damn you, Heather Tomasi," he groaned. "Get out from under my skin!"

"Where is April?"

Rob stared at Heather. That was one very angry woman standing on his doorstep.

"At Sylvia and Eric's," he answered. "Why?" He'd never suspected that brown eyes could hold so much ice.

"Good. I don't believe in exposing children to violence."

His eyebrows rose. "Violence?"

"Yes, dammit, violence! The same kind of violence you perpetrated at the jumpsite not an hour ago! You *hit* somebody!" She took a step into his doorway. He backed up.

"You hit a paying customer of my company! He's

talking about suing! He can take us for everything we have! What the hell got into you? And what were you doing there anyway?"

Rob hauled her the rest of the way through the door, wondering how she had found his house so fast. "I was invited, remember?"

He kicked the door shut, then sucked in a long breath. She smelled good. Of forest and moss and woman and the outdoors. She looked wonderful, dressed in narrow-leg jeans and a red sweatshirt with her company logo on it, encircling a stylized web with a black spider in the center. He pulled her closer.

"And I bought a ticket so you could entertain me along with all those yahoos. I supported your business. Helped make your exhibition a paying proposition, so what's your objection, lady?"

Her breasts, heaving as she panted, touched his chest. She felt fantastic too. Warm and soft and female. He wanted her like he'd never wanted another woman in his life. He ached with it, was so hard he thought he might burst.

Oblivious, she thrust herself out of his hold. "Dammit, your ticket didn't entitle you to pop another paying customer and knock him unconscious. He and his pal are *loggers*, for heaven's sake!"

"So? What the hell was I supposed to do? Call him out? Offer to meet him at dawn with chain saws drawn?" He grinned without humor. "He'd win any kind of a duel like that, then he'd probably try to sue me because he'd dulled his blade on my bones."

She made a disgusted face. "You may think this is some kind of a joke, McGee, but loggers are tough guys! They can be dangerous when aroused."

"And so can I." He grabbed her by the shoulders and barely restrained the urge to shake her. "Logger or not, his ticket didn't entitle him to make lewd comments about your naked body!"

She slapped her forearms up, fists clenched, and dislodged his hands. "Like hell it didn't! I knew there'd be comments like that. I factored that in when I was deciding whether or not to do it. I couldn't hear the comments, and if I had, I wouldn't have taken them personally."

"I could hear them!" he bellowed, he who never treated women anything but gently, he who never raised his voice, knowing that sweet reason was more effective than macho tirades. "I *did* hear them. And I didn't like them. *I* took them personally."

"Personally? Why?"

"I don't know why, but I did and—" He broke off. His brows pulled in in so tight a frown, it made his head ache. He rubbed his forehead, trying to ease the tension. It didn't work, and he went back on the offensive.

"And how the hell did you know it was *me* who smacked that yutz anyway? You couldn't have seen that. You couldn't have even known I was there. I didn't leave my card."

It was her turn to frown. She backed up a step or two. "I . . ." She blinked. "I don't know. I just . . . knew. It had to be you. I mean, who else would have . . ." Her tongue touched her parted lips, first the top one, then the bottom. Then her teeth sank into the lower one and Rob was lost.

Groaning, he dragged her against him, buried his hands in her thick, lush hair, and kissed her rosy red lips, his tongue driving between them and staking a claim, making a demand, forcing a response.

He got one.

She lifted her knee and jabbed it toward his groin, and he instinctively twisted, blocking her. He didn't realize until it was all over and he was flat on his back on the floor, staring up at her, that she'd anticipated exactly that move on his part. She'd counted on it, used his movement as the basis for hers.

She stood over him, her fists clenched, her eyes ablaze, her chest heaving.

"You want to kiss me, mister, you ask. You don't grab. You don't take. You don't make sudden moves that might frighten me. Got it?"

Lithely, hiding the wince that would have told her she'd done more damage than he wanted her to know about, he rose to his feet. "Got it," he said, and moved in close again.

"Ms. Tomasi, I want to kiss you."

Her breath left her in a rush. He saw her swallow. "You . . . do?" Her startled eyes asked silently, *Still?*

He touched her neck gently and smiled. "I do. Very, very much. May I?" He couldn't remember ever having said something like that before, but the ground rules had been laid down and he found he enjoyed following them. Want—*need*—hammered in his blood, made more potent by this restraint she demanded of him.

His polite request might have been responsible for the hint of disappointment he detected in her expression. Had she expected him to overwhelm her, to overrule her? Fight with her?

Then she shrugged as if it were of no interest to her whether he kissed her. "I suppose you could."

He wrapped his fingers over the point of her shoulder, feeling bone and tense muscle and warm skin through her shirt, slid his other hand to the small of her back, and drew her slowly, carefully, against him. She was hot. He was hot. Their combined heat threatened spontaneous combustion. Fine tremors rippled through the flesh under his hands.

"Ah, but supposing isn't good enough," he said. "Do you want me to?"

She drew a deep breath and let it trickle out. "I don't . . . not want you to."

He felt as if she had handed him a partial victory. "Am I frightening you?"

She smiled. He suspected she meant it to be lofty, but he sensed again a hint of excitement bubbling beneath her calm surface. "Of course you're not frightening me. Maybe I used the wrong term. I should have warned you not to startle me. You don't—men don't—scare me at all."

He touched his lips to hers, just a whisper of contact, and felt them quiver. "You scare me, lady. You scare the living bejesus out of me."

As if his admission gave her courage, her arms came up slowly, palms gliding over his chest, fingers touching his throat before slipping to the back of his neck and threading into his hair. "Why?" she whispered.

"Why what?"

"Why do you want to kiss me? And why does it scare you?"

He smiled into her eyes, feeling shivers of fear and excitement racing the length of her body. "You know the answer to both those questions. And you're just as scared."

For a moment, he thought she might deny it, then she sighed. "God . . . yes," she breathed, and he felt the breath against his lips, tremulous, hot, moist. "How did you know?"

"The same way you knew it was me who couldn't let a mouthy lout get away with comments about you. We're connected, Heather Tomasi. Connected in all sorts of ways we don't even know about yet. But we will. We'll learn. Together."

"No." She shook her head and her hair whispered across his wrist. He turned his hand over and captured a fistful of its silk. "I just want you for a month."

"A month? That won't be enough."

"It will have to be," she said, and he heard something almost desperate in her voice.

He smiled. "Not nearly enough. And I can see that you know it." He looked at her long and searchingly before he kissed her eyelids, closing them.

He trailed his lips down her face to her throat, pressing them to the wild pulse in the hollow there as she tilted her head back. "I can feel it.

"And I can taste it," he said seconds later against her mouth. He traced the outline of her lips with the tip of his tongue, then lifted his head.

Her lids looked heavy, her lashes fluttered. The pulse in her throat was going insane. She swayed toward him, seeking. "Rob . . . Robbie . . . ?"

He filtered his hand through her hair, letting it fall. "What do you want?"

"Why did you stop?"

"Kissing you?"

"Yes."

"Because I don't want to . . . startle you. I want you to be prepared."

Her eyes glittered with a hint of temper. "You want me to ask."

He chuckled. He couldn't help it. Lord, but making love to her was going to be fun. Among other things. "So perceptive," he said. "Are you?"

She was cool. On the surface. "Asking?"

"Yes."

"Robbie . . ." He thought he could get accustomed, very quickly, to hearing her call him that. It sounded right. Ordinarily he hated it, corrected women who so presumed. "Kiss me."

This time, he didn't startle her, but he did get a response.

It started deep inside her. As it grew, pulsing, burning, turning her limbs to lead, Heather knew that it had really started two years ago, and that this time nothing was going to stop it from running its full course.

Donald had been wrong. She wasn't frigid. Gerald hadn't ruined her.

She trembled with need and fear, and she wanted whatever this was with Rob to be finished right now. Before she got hurt.

His scent swept over her. His taste engulfed her. His body surged against hers, hot and hard. She sent her hands on a journey of exploration, sliding inside the open front of his shirt, her fingers spreading across his shoulders, down to his chest, tangling in the thick mat of hair. His mouth moved over hers, his tongue thrusting, finding hers, flicking against it, teasing, tangling, in a delicious dance of advance and retreat. She felt what might be a sob rising up in her chest, but it became a soft, aching moan and she released it.

It trembled from her, against his lips, and she heard him answer with a deep, male sound. His arms held her so tightly, she thought she couldn't breathe, but it ceased to matter. She was insubstantial, floating on a wave of warmth, needing no air in her lungs to sustain life. It entered through her every pore.

His hands roved over her back and down her buttocks, molding her to him, pressing her against the rigid rod of his sex. She raked her fingers down his chest, finding one of his nipples, and spent a long, fascinated time rotating the heel of her hand over it.

He took his mouth from hers and kissed under her chin, below her ear, tugged the neck of her sweatshirt aside and kissed along her collar bone. When he laid his open mouth on the pulse she felt hammering in her throat, she choked back another moan. His tongue, hot and wet, pressed in rhythm with her blood as his fingers, curved under her buttocks, sent the same inescapable cadence through her lower body.

This time, the sob of pure ecstasy escaped.

At once, he lifted his head, his eyes glazed as he looked at her. He relaxed his fingers, sliding them to the small of her back. She saw him dimly, through a strange blur.

"Heather!" His voice was filled with concern. "Did I hurt you?"

She shook her head, unable to speak. He cradled

the back of her head in one hand and brushed his lips over her cheeks. "You're crying."

Bewildered, disbelieving, she shook her head again, despite the moisture she now felt on her cheeks. "No . . ." The denial was foolish, but one she had to make. She had no reason to cry. She laughed, but it came out all choked and ragged. "I'm not. Truly I'm not."

Inside, she was singing. *I'm not made of ice! Truly I'm not.* She could feel. She could feel all the things she had once felt and then forgotten how to feel. Or learned how not to. With Rob, she could feel them again.

It was as wonderful as it was scary.

"Yes," he said. "These are tears." He touched them with a finger, wiping them up and carrying them to her mouth. "Taste. Salty."

She cupped his hand in her own, lapping the drop of moisture from his finger tip with one pass of her tongue. Then, prodded by an instinct she couldn't disobey, she sucked gently. He shuddered against her and groaned. To her consternation, tears spurted from her eyes again. *He had liked that!*

She dropped his hand and stepped back, wariness bringing caution to the surface.

"I don't know what's happening to me," she said, trying to smile as she scrubbed at her face with the backs of her hands. "I'm sorry." Her throat ached. She wished she were alone so she could cry in earnest, she who almost never cried. It was as if a huge ball of something hard and sharp hid inside her, and the only way to release it was with tears. "I'm sorry," she repeated. Blinking her eyes clear, she met his gaze to show him she was fine.

He brushed her hands aside and ran his thumbs over her cheeks, removing the last traces of moisture. She hoped he wouldn't insist on knowing why she had cried. She wasn't sure she even knew herself. Were tears a part of relief? And hadn't that relief been premature? She shuddered again, thinking of the raw passion of their kisses. That had definitely been premature.

"Do you know what you look like now?" His voice was rough edged with tension. Did desire continue to pulse through him as it did her? Did fires still rage deep inside him, merely banked for the time being? What would happen if she let them roar out of control? What would happen to her? What would happen to him?

She shook her head.

"You look the way you did when you finished the pumpkin pie yesterday."

She stepped back from him and ran her hands down the front of her sweatshirt. "What? Fat?" she asked with a laugh, managing to get a tenuous grip on her runaway emotions.

His lips twitched. "The words *Heather* and *fat* are not synonymous. You look . . ." He paused and ran a hand into his hair. "*Looked* as if you'd never before in your life had anything as sweet as those kisses."

She took another step back. Lord! Was the man prescient? If he'd asked her to describe their first kisses, those would have been her very words.

She laughed again, wondering where she'd been keeping all that presence of mind. Why hadn't she been able to find it when she really needed it, when those ridiculous tears were spurting? "Kissing you was an extremely pleasant pursuit."

Devastating was more like it, but there was no way she was going to let him know that. Because it shouldn't have devastated her. She was a big girl now. No way should a man disturb her to the point that she couldn't control her responses. That was a lesson she'd learned the hard way, and she intended never to forget it.

He moved in on her again, smiling. "It was extremely pleasant for me too. If you liken our shared kisses to desserts, do you plan to pig out today as well?"

"Yesterday, I was starved for desserts."

"Today, I'm starved for kisses."

She backed up and ran smack into a wall. She gave him a cool look that should have warned him off. His grin told her that while he might be alerted to possible danger, he wasn't feeling cautious.

Her heart rate increased to aerobic heights. Could this kind of activity actually be good for her? It was a wondrous thought. "And you?" he asked. "What are you starved for today?"

"Breakfast," she said. Even aerobic exercise could be overdone. "I never eat before I jump."

His thighs brushed hers. "I suppose you want me to feed you?"

Which appetite did he refer to? The one she didn't want stirred up again. There was no question of that.

Simply thinking about it heightened her craving for more of what he had. If she didn't move away from the warmth of his body, that hunger would be out of control again in a moment. But where could she go, with a wall at her back?

She brazened it out. "Are you offering to feed me?"

He dipped his head. His breath caressed her cheek.

"Oh, yes," he said. "Open your mouth, Heather. Take what I give."

She wanted it. Despite all her misgivings, despite the certainty that this was the worst possible action she could take, she wanted it so badly that she opened her mouth and received him.

He gave and she took, and then, with her heart pounding, her lungs burning, she gave and he took. They made low, gratified sounds together. His mouth hardened. Hers softened. His tongue chased, hers retreated until they played turnabout and reversed the process. It was wild, heady, exquisite pleasure, pleasure that invaded the deepest reaches of her body. Heather felt again the kind of excitement she had wanted to forget, but she was powerless to stop the surges within.

He could take no more. Rob knew it. It was either stop now, or not at all. He tore his mouth from hers and pressed her cheek to his chest. Her breath came damp and fast against his skin as he simply held her, finding an aching pleasure in that too. He turned so that his back was to the wall and she rested against him. Her breathing slowed, almost stopped, then she drew in another deep, tremulous breath.

He cupped her chin and tilted her face up to his. Her eyes showed the same dazed, incredulous expression as before, but this time there were no tears, only questions.

He didn't have the answers, but he found himself more and more willing to find them. Skimming his mouth across her face, he closed her eyes with soft kisses, reveled in the peachy down that dusted her cheeks, explored the satin of her skin. "Heather . . ."

She didn't open her eyes, simply rested her head against his shoulder, face turned up to him, body warm and soft and trembling between his spread legs. "What?"

"Tell me to stop."

Her lips curved in a smile he longed to kiss. Her tongue came out and moistened them so that they glistened temptingly. "Stop."

He held himself back, pounding with the need to give into that temptation and prolonging the pleasure of waiting to do it. "You didn't say it with much conviction," he accused gently, lifting the hem of her sweatshirt. She wore a thinner top under that. He tugged it out of the waistband of her jeans and ran his hand up her back. The skin there felt as beautiful as it had looked in the morning sun, felt as delectable as it had when they'd danced at that long-ago wedding reception. He raked his nails lightly down her spine from her bra to the waist of her jeans, then followed her jeans around to the front. He slid his palm upward until he cupped a breast and felt her shudder. He lifted, squeezed gently. She shuddered again and leaned more heavily against him as she whispered softly, so softly, "Robbie . . ."

He knew in that moment that if he'd lifted her in his arms and carried her to the bedroom, she'd have gone willingly. She'd have been his. They'd have been one.

For the life of him, Rob didn't know why, but that delicate, yearning response of hers, that sighing submission to what was slowly killing them both, was what stopped him. It stopped him as surely as if she'd been a frightened young virgin who needed more time.

Pulling her shirts back down, he held her, rocking her back and forth. He jerked his head up as the front door was flung open and April ran in, with Sylvia close behind. Heather tried to leap away from him, but he caught her arms and held her in front of him, his body pressed against her back, his arousal hidden.

Sylvia grinned at Heather. "Well! Fancy meeting you here! I take it this means you asked him? And that he agreed?"

As she spoke, April stared up at Rob, then at Heather. "She doesn't get to ask him, Sylvia," the girl said. "He has to ask her." Her face aglow with excitement and the animation he'd long missed seeing in her, she looked at Rob again. "Did you, Uncle Robbie? Ask her, I mean? Is Heather the one? Is she going to be your new wife?"

Four

Heather's knees, already weak, threatened to cave in entirely. She clutched the side of the bookcase and swiveled her head around to stare at Rob.

"Wife?" Her voice was hoarse, overly loud, but it didn't quite drown out his emphatic "No!" They stared at each other, equally appalled.

Sylvia broke the pulsating silence. "We, uh, came to see if you wanted to join us for Sunday brunch, Rob. You, too, of course, Heather, since you're here. Eric and the babies are out in the car. We'd like to take April. She's a wonderful baby-sitter, entertains them so well and—"

She broke off, obviously having read Rob's expression. "No, huh?"

Rob shook his head.

"I'll go!" Heather tried to lunge forward, but only staggered a tiny step before his hands on her upper arms stopped her.

"You're invited for breakfast here, remember?"

She blinked, swallowed hard, and nodded. "Oh. Right. I . . . forgot." *What are you doing?* a demented little voice cried inside her. *Get out of here! Now!* She twisted to look at him again. Wife? His niece thought he was looking for a wife? He met her gaze, his expression bland. Slowly, as he released her arms, she stepped away from him.

It was all right, she told herself. Of course it was. He'd said no, hadn't he? April was just a little kid. They made mistakes about what the adults around them intended. A man who wanted a wife wouldn't have just spent the past ten minutes kissing *her* until they were both weak and shaking, would he? Of course not.

"Another time," Sylvia said, her gaze flicking from Rob to Heather. She draped an arm around April. "Come on, honey bun. I really need you along to help with Shanna and Shane."

After Sylvia and April had left, Heather walked unsteadily across the room to sit in a big, squashy chair that smelled new. She leaned her head back and closed her eyes. To her shock, she was still trembling so hard she had to clench her jaws to keep her teeth from chattering.

Rob watched her struggle for control, then crouched before her. He placed his hands on the seat beside her, close to her hips, but not touching. "Breakfast, Ms. Tomasi," he said. "I think your blood sugar is down."

She pulled in a deep breath and sat up straight as she looked at him. For a moment her mouth trembled, but she firmed it and said, "You may be right, Doctor." Her hands still shook as she reached out and carefully buttoned his shirt, refusing to meet his eyes.

He stood when she was done and held out a hand to help her up. She took it, and he winced at her grip.

"Oh!" she said, turning his hand over and staring at his split, swollen, and bruised knuckles. "Oh, Rob." She looked up at him, her eyes filled with reproach as well as regret. "Damn fool," she said, but it came out sounding like an endearment.

He shrugged, his gaze fixed on his large hand resting on her smaller one, palm to palm. The fingers of her other hand traced the outline of the bruise, scarcely touching, not hurting, possibly healing.

"What a dumb thing for a surgeon to do." A glimmer of humor lurked in her eyes. "Something like a logger deliberately dulling his chain saw. On somebody else's bones."

Reluctantly, he grinned. The tools of his trade—his hands—had never been likened to a chain saw before.

"Maybe I could sue the other guy for having such a hard jaw," he said.

"And maybe you should let the whole thing drop." She frowned, letting go of his hand. For a moment, she looked as if she might be considering socking him. "If you sue, it'll be as good as an admission of guilt. Then everybody will know the identity of the mysterious defender of my honor."

He raised one eyebrow. "You mean they don't? You didn't share your suspicions?"

She shrugged with one shoulder as she held up her hands palms up. "What can I say? I took into consideration the fact that you're a newcomer here and might not know our ways."

"How generous of you."

Her mouth quirked in a quick smile. "As you said, what I had were 'suspicions.' Any accusation I made publicly would have been pure supposition on my part. I didn't see you punch the man."

He gave a sagacious nod. "This is true."

"And besides, you'd paid your money, the same as he had. If he's entitled to get his entertainment value out of my morning's work, then maybe you were too."

"Of course," he said solemnly. "I like to see things all neatly justified, so everyone's happy." His eyes flickered teasingly. "But what about your partners? Won't they want the publicity your silence is costing Aer-Real Adventures? Can't you see the headlines? 'Army Officer Runs Amok at Nude Bungee-Jumping Site. Uses Commando Training to Deck Innocent Spectator.'"

She folded her arms across her chest as if suffering a sudden chill. Her eyes were wide. "Commando training?"

He draped his arm around her shoulders and turned her toward the kitchen. "No. But newspapers love to call army types 'commandos' and blame their brutal training for their every infraction. Haven't you seen it? 'Former soldier runs red light. Ex-commando callously risks life of mother-to-be. Shaken woman says, "If I hadn't stopped to window-shop, I'd have been in that crosswalk."'"

Heather laughed and slipped free of his arm. It was hot in his house with the sun beating in through undraped windows. She stripped her sweatshirt off and shook her hair down again over shoulders bared by a tank top. "You're exaggerating."

"Only a bit," he said, and continued to exaggerate only a bit with tales of military life, which he clearly loved. He didn't, she noticed, tell her any of the wild exploits involving women that Eric had mentioned.

To her amusement, because she'd been expecting a playboy-on-the-morning-after show-off meal like eggs Benedict or expertly flipped French omelets and champagne in the orange juice, he served sliced cantaloupe and hot cereal. He set her bowl in front of her and encouraged her to eat it all. "That's the most nutritious breakfast you could possibly get," he said, "and you need to make up lost ground after last night's dinner."

To defy him, she added an extra spoonful of brown sugar.

Over her empty oatmeal bowl she asked, finally, the question she'd been wanting to since hearing of the fisticuffs on the cliff top. "Why *did* you go to the jump, Rob?"

His gaze was steady on her face, but it hid things. "I couldn't sleep."

She waited a moment before saying, "Counting sheep doesn't cost a hundred bucks."

His lips twitched at one corner, a travesty of a smile. "Maybe not, but it wasn't effective. I thought seeing you . . . at work would be."

She didn't have to ask, Effective in what way? She knew. They shared a troubled look. She lowered her eyes first.

"Why did you come here?" he asked softly, bringing her gaze back to him. "That guy can't possibly nail your company for something completely beyond your control, and you know it."

She also knew he didn't need her to answer that

question. It was evident by what had happened within moments of her arrival, by the way she'd succumbed after her initial resistance. And then, she hadn't been resisting him as much as his methods. Still, she tried to deny it, lying to herself and to him. "I didn't come for . . . what happened. Really, Rob."

"No?" His mocking gaze told her he didn't buy the lie any more than she did. "What then? What is it you said yesterday you 'needed' me for? That Sylvia thought this morning you'd already asked me?"

Restless, she rose and paced to the back door. It stood open to the warmth of the sun, admitting the sweet scent of honeysuckle. She pushed on the screen and stepped out onto the narrow gray-painted stoop. The screen door slammed shut behind her, forming a poor barrier between them. "I changed my mind about needing you for anything, remember?"

He shouldered the door open and came after her. She skipped down the two shallow steps to the cracked sidewalk and strode to the far end of the backyard, until a sagging picket fence stopped her. On her right was a yard with the honeysuckle she'd smelled, spilling over an arbor. On her left was another yard with two ten-speed bikes, a badminton net, and a rusty barbecue. Both were separated from her by that same picket fence.

She bent and picked a spent blossom off a bedraggled rose bush. "I decided you weren't the kind of man I needed after all." She nipped another dead rose free and dropped it to the untended ground near the back fence.

He didn't, as she had feared, approach any closer, but stayed on the stoop, sitting with his elbows resting on splayed knees. The dappled shade of a ginkgo tree filtered over him, so that sun gilded his hair in patches, shade darkened it in others, and his expression was obscured as he watched her.

"What kind of man do you need?" His voice, not loud, nevertheless carried to her and seemed to thrum against something inside her. Need. It swept over her in a wash as inexorable as an incoming tide. In his arms, she had experienced need. He was the second man to make her feel that way, that helpless.

Never again.

"I don't *need* any kind of man at all," she said. "I'm an adult. I don't need a man to validate my existence."

"Yes. You made that point. You don't run after men or buses." He didn't run after women, either, Rob thought. He frowned, remembering yesterday when he'd followed Heather twice, and remembering this morning, when he'd followed her to the canyon.

His only consolation was that she had followed him home. Whatever was going on here, he wasn't in it alone. But then, he'd known that two years ago. And he'd walked away from it. This time, he didn't think there was anywhere to go.

"What kind of man do you want?" He stressed the last word, unintentionally making his question sound faintly derisive.

She didn't answer as she walked back across the yard, running her hand along the picket fence. She stopped at the gate that led to his unfenced front yard.

"I don't want any kind," she said, fixing her gaze on him. "Not personally. It's for my parents' sake I have to . . . would like to, well, give the appearance of having one for the month they're home on vacation." She leaned on the fence, one hand on the gate. "A proper, conservative gentleman. I try to have one for them every year."

"What?" Rob had to laugh at the notion of Heather Tomasi needing a proper, conservative anything for any length of time. "What in the world do you want someone like that for?"

"Because that's what they want for me."

"Why?"

Her smile was wry. "They want me to settle down."

Rob watched her as she clicked the latch and opened the gate, then held on to it, swinging it back and forth, fanning the grass he would cut as soon as he bought a lawn mower.

Domestic needs, he thought. Unaccustomed domestic needs, like tables and chairs and linens. And a wife. Things he'd never needed before. Always before, everything had been laid on.

Even the women, it sometimes seemed. But never a wife. He looked at Heather, wanting her more and more. As a *wife*?

He laughed again. "And as you said, you have no intention of settling down."

"None whatsoever. That's why I thought you'd be ideal. You're like me, but they wouldn't know that. They'd see the uniform, the rank, the degree in medicine. They could believe in you, respect you, a medical doctor like my father, and we could all enjoy their time home without dissent to upset my grandparents. Grandpa has ulcers."

"And what about next year, when the man you take on to impress them this summer is out of the picture?"

He heard genuine amusement in her laughter, but not enough to disguise a surprising tinge of sorrow.

"Next year? By then, they'll have forgotten you— the man—completely, just as they'll have put me out of their minds until their annual visit home forces them to remember me. And then they'll again be volubly disappointed that I'm still unmarried, still childless, still 'wasting my time.'"

"What do they do? Where do they live?"

"They run a medical mission in Ecuador. Mom's an ordained minister, and like I said, Dad's a doctor. That's why they'd have seen you as the ideal man for me."

"That's a switch." He couldn't hide the irony. "Anyway, why wouldn't I do for your purposes? Don't you think I could act the part of a proper, conservative gentleman, even for a month?"

"Yes, but . . ." She shrugged, looking away from him.

There were other considerations that she obviously wasn't willing to bring up. They both knew what they were. They both knew why she needed to be outside his house right now with her hand on an open gate.

"Such a shame," he said, "that the guy with the pony tail is your ex. I'm certain a minister-mother would welcome a man of the cloth as a son-in-law. You shouldn't have broken up with him."

"Alvin?" Her eyes opened wide for a second, then squinted almost shut as laughter bubbled out of her throat. It sounded bright and shiny as it danced across the yard in the golden sun. "Yikes, he'd have set them off like no one ever has! I'd have had to hide him if we were still going together. They'd hate to see me with someone like him. And he's no more a man of the cloth than you are. That's an affectation. If he has an ordination, it's one he bought out of the back of a cheap magazine."

Rob chuckled. "I assure you, my medical qualifications are genuine, as is my rank." Something prodded him to insist. "Let me help, Heather. After all, it's only for a month. What harm can come of making your parents happy for that long?"

Right, he thought, it was only a month. He could surely put April's needs on hold for that long. After all, he didn't anticipate being posted somewhere else for at least another two years, and he'd already enrolled April in an after-school program at the local library. When school was out for the summer, she'd be going to her grandmother, making this courting business easier.

Heather left the gate ajar and returned to the stoop, sitting beside him, but well apart. "I don't think so, thanks all the same. But never mind. It's my own fault and it's not your problem. I go through the same thing, scrambling to find someone suitable every year."

She gave him a sidelong look. "It's really quite strange, because when I first asked Sylvia for help, because she knows so many people, she claimed there was no one appropriate." She smiled faintly. "She's still a little ticked off with me because of an airline pilot who completely misunderstood things and refused to go away nicely when he was no longer needed. He was hard to get rid of."

Rob remembered being tossed to the floor. "What did you do to get rid of him?"

She shrugged. "He finally . . . gave up. But do

you know what he wanted? After a week, a *week*, mind you, he wanted me to marry him!"

Rob let his mouth hang open for a moment. "How . . . perverted."

A dirty look accompanied her "Sarcasm, I don't need. You know what I mean," she continued. "How would you feel if some woman came on all moonlight and roses and started talking love and marriage after you'd known her for a week?" She didn't wait for him to reply. "You'd run, too, like I did."

"Hmm." He nodded. "So go on. I take it Sylvia decided to forgive you for the airline pilot and help you find someone."

"No. Not really. When there was no one available immediately, I got very brave and daring and convinced myself that I really should go it alone this year, let my parents fret and fume at me all they want. Then you arrived and she insisted I had to meet you again." Heather smiled ruefully. "She persuaded me that you'd be perfect."

He wondered if Sylvia had told her that he, too, had asked for help, if Heather knew what *he* wanted *her* for.

Her? He brought himself up short. What was he thinking of? He didn't want *her* for that! It would be more than folly to want her as a wife. It would be as crazy as jumping off her bungee bridge. Without the elastics.

"And now you don't think I would be perfect?" he said with mock injured feelings.

She looked at him, long and thoroughly, then, to his amazement, she blushed and glanced away. "No, I don't."

Something leapt inside him. What if . . .

He caught her chin and turned her face toward his, his heart beating much too fast. Her cheeks were pink and her breathing uneven, but she met his eyes with a steady look, one that told him unequivocally that any *what ifs* should be kept completely to himself. "Why not?" he asked.

His thumb glided over her chin, rode up along her jawline to her cheekbone, enjoying the texture of her skin. His gaze slid slowly over her face in its wake. He was enchanted by the play of light and shadow across her features, excited almost unbearably by the watchfulness in her eyes, the fluttering of her pulse in her throat.

"Be-because," she said, her voice nothing more than a shaken whisper.

He bent and touched his mouth to hers, felt her lips quiver, heard her soft sigh. As he tasted the sweetness of her, he slid a hand into her hair, holding the back of her head. Something about the feel of her hair tantalized him, made him want to touch it again and again, to wrap himself in it, to breathe in its perfume, to immerse his face in it.

He closed his eyes and continued to hold her lightly, their lips barely touching, until he thought he'd go mad with wanting more. But she didn't offer it and he didn't take it. He lifted his head, slipped his hand away, and sat back, leaning his elbows on the step behind him. He did wrap the fingers of his left hand loosely around her wrist, and he could feel her pulse, wild, erratic, disturbed. Disturbing.

She looked at him for a minute longer, then got to her feet. She was gone out the open gate, shutting it behind her, before he realized her intentions. By the time he reached the fence, her car was pulling away from the curb.

She gave a cheerful little toot of the horn as she left.

"Well," Sylvia said to Heather when she arrived at the health club for her Wednesday-morning workout. "What was going on Sunday morning between you and Uncle Robbie? It looked . . ." She seemed to be searching for the right word. "Intense? Interesting?" She grinned. "I'm only guessing, of course. You tell me what it was."

Heather shrugged. "It wasn't," she said dismissively. "Either."

"But it will get that way, I'm betting. When are you seeing him again?"

"I'm not."

Heather stabbed the button that turned on the music to begin the workout, leaving Sylvia with no choice but to take her place in the class. As she put the group through their paces with perhaps a trifle more energy than any of them thought was necessary, she wished she could steer her friend in some other direction. Once Sylvia's curiosity was aroused, though, she'd pick and pick until she had the whole story. If it involved any other man, Heather might have been willing to share, but not that man. And not that time.

Nothing, she promised herself, was going to make her divulge any of the confusion she'd lived with since Sunday. Sylvia would laugh. And she'd insist on hearing not only the nitty, but the gritty too.

Fine, Heather decided, leading her troop outside

for a three-mile run now that they were nicely warmed up. Sylvia could ask all she wanted. Heather would "just say no."

Of course, it wasn't that easy.

"All right," Sylvia said after the session, sidling up to Heather at the juice bar. "Give! What's going on with you and Rob?"

Heather clenched her jaw and glanced at a group of customers leaning on the bar, any of whom might be listening to her private agony bruited about. "I told you," she whispered. "Nothing."

Sylvia raised her brows. "Nothing? That didn't look like nothing to me, friend. The man was as horn—"

Heather grasped Sylvia's wrist in a tight grip. "Keep your voice down, will you?"

"Sure." Sylvia grinned. "If you'll tell me what's up."

"Nothing's up. Will you drop the subject? It's none of your affair."

"None of my affair? Since when haven't we shared our problems?"

"Please, please, just leave it, will you? There are no problems to share. What makes you think there are problems?" It was almost a wail.

Sylvia steered Heather to a corner table.

"Hey, come on," she said cajolingly, and Heather knew Sylvia was more worried about her than interested in gossip for gossip's sake. "My best friend looks like somebody's cut her legs out from under her, and you say it's none of my affair?" She shoved Heather onto a chair and plopped down opposite her. "You're hurting over something, Heather, and I don't like to see that." She clutched the ends of the towel she had draped around her neck. "I'm the one who introduced you to the guy. I feel responsible."

Heather shoved her hair back from her face. "Well, don't. There's nothing going on between me and Rob McGee."

"No? You reportedly spent a long time locked in the downstairs biffy with him at my party. And after dinner I was there while he sat like a stone on the ground, turning whiter and whiter each time you mentioned the bungee thing. His jaw muscles clenched so hard I thought he was going to break molars."

Heather set her bottle of mineral water down on the table with unnecessary force. "So, he disapproves of naked bungee jumping. That's not my problem, Syl."

"But you had a problem with him. He left April with us Saturday night and leapt in his car, driving like a maniac, about five minutes after you pulled out. Then Eric says you phoned in an absolute rage about seven-thirty Sunday morning, demanding to know Rob's address. Later, when we arrive to see if he's still alive, what do we find but the two of you obviously coming out of a steamy clinch."

Heather looked at her and sipped her mineral water. "So? He socked one of my customers. We had a fight about it. Then we kissed and made up. And I left and we won't be seeing each other again unless it's by accident. There. That's the whole story. Are you satisfied now? I hope so, because there's nothing more to know."

Sylvia threw up her hands in disgust. "You're impossible! Those aren't even the high points of the whole story. I want to know what's going on. I want to know what happened Saturday night after you left my place. I want to know why you get that awful, closed look on your face when I so much as mention his name. Rob," she said deliberately. "Rob McGee."

Heather squeezed her eyes shut and shoved back from the table. Leaping up, she spun away and marched into her office. Sylvia followed, shouldering her way in before Heather could shut the door.

"Hey, what's wrong?"

Heather flung herself into her swivel chair and buried her face in her arms on her desk. "I don't know!" she cried. "I don't know, and I'm too damned scared to find out!"

"It doesn't surprise me to know that your parents worry about you," Rob said when Heather walked back to solid ground at the end of the catwalk. It was Thursday afternoon. He hadn't seen her since Sunday, and none of her impact on him had diminished. "You shouldn't have been left on the loose this long." He had just watched her jump, fully clothed, and the terror for her safety had also been undiminished by the passage of time either.

"It surprises me," she said. Clearly, she wasn't referring to his presence there.

He took her arm, trying to ignore the three men—her partners, he assumed—who watched the two of them from the center of the catwalk. "What surprises you?" he asked. "The length of time you've been on the loose?"

She gave him a level look. "That my parents waste time worrying about me for even one month of the year. I'm thirty-two years old. I've been looking after myself for a long time." Abruptly, she changed the subject.

"Did you come to jump? If so, you should be talking to one of the others. I'm off duty now. Or you can phone the office tomorrow and make arrangements for a session on the weekend. Jumping is done for the day."

He shook his head. "I already phoned the office. A nice woman named Ellie told me you were here. I didn't come to jump. I told you I like my adventures right side up. I came to talk to you."

She slipped her arm free, tilted one shoulder up for a second as if shrugging him off, then walked away along the path, her hands in the back pockets of her jeans. She glanced at him over her shoulder. "About?"

He followed her. "Your parents, I suppose," he said, suddenly unsure exactly why he was there. Except . . . he had to be there. "And how I can help."

Taking her hands out of her pockets, she trotted down a flight of stairs made from rough-cut cedar. "They're my problem, not yours, and I don't want your help. It won't kill them to fret about me for a single month of the year. Or me to have to listen to lectures."

He caught up with her at the bottom of the stairs and walked beside her as the path widened. "A single month?" He worried about April all the time. "Parents worry about their kids constantly. I'm sure they've been doing it all your life."

"No." For just an instant, he spotted a hint of bleakness in her eyes. She shrugged that one shoulder again and the fleeting impression of melancholy was swept away as she smiled with affection.

"My parents are like absentminded professors. They only concern themselves with me when they're face-to-face with the fact that they have a daughter."

He caught her arm in one hand. His fingers moved slowly along the inner surface of her wrist. Lord, but she had wonderful skin. "What makes you so sure they don't worry about you when they're away?"

She tugged her arm free. "They have much more important things to concern themselves with. The natives they care for comprise their family—except when they come home. Then they remember they have me. And they fret because I'm not doing what girls are supposed to do."

"You're an only child?" He thought of how important April had become to him since she'd been in his care. "They have a right to their concerns, Heather. You're their little girl. They only want you to be safe."

"I haven't been anybody's little girl for a long time, and I don't need a man to 'keep me safe.'"

"Why *don't* you find someone permanent?" he asked. "That way, you wouldn't have to scramble around every year to find someone to pretend with."

They had reached the parking lot, and she walked to a white van with her company logo on it. She leaned against the driver's door, arms folded across her chest, one foot in front of the other. She looked at him steadily, a faintly derisive smile on her face. "You mean a husband."

"You say that like it gives you a bad taste in your mouth."

"Maybe it does. I've already tried it, thanks. Marriage isn't an acquired taste, like anchovy pizza.

Either you like it at the first bite, or you don't, and that's not subject to change. I didn't like it any more than you would."

Something in him raged at the thought of her having been married. Why had she hated it? What had been wrong with the guy that she hadn't been happy? What— He cut off the mental questions with an oral one. "How do you know I wouldn't like it?"

"You mean you would?" There was open amusement in her tone. "You told April no, when she asked."

"I told April no, you aren't the one."

She only looked at him blankly, waiting. "All right," he said, "so I *don't* want one—anyone." Hell, he sounded as sullen as a fourteen-year-old facing inoculations. "The fact is, I need a wife. I have to find one."

"You?" Air escaped her lungs. She dragged in a deep breath and tried to let it out easy, but it erupted on a burst of laughter. "You need a wife?"

"Me. I need a wife."

Five

Heather couldn't believe what she'd heard. She slumped back against the door of the van, arms wrapped around her middle, and stared at him through laughter-induced tears.

"Why?"

"Because April needs a mother. That means I need a wife."

She laughed some more.

"I'm serious about this!" he said. "Dammit, it's not so funny. I'm thirty-seven years old. Why shouldn't I be thinking about getting married?"

Serious? He was. Lord, he was! "I . . . well . . . " She opened the door of the van and sat on the end of the seat with her feet out, regarding him through the open window. "You've got a well-deserved name as a dedicated bachelor."

"Had," he corrected her, glowering. "*Had* a name. And maybe it wasn't as well-deserved as people like to think."

She canted one eyebrow upward. "Eric lived with you, Rob. I don't suppose there's anything wrong with his powers of observation. And Sylvia told me how reluctant April's grandmother was to let her visit you, because of your 'carrying on' with women."

He gave her a baleful look down his nose. "So reluctant. But who has April now? And that, when it comes down to it, is why I need a wife. And soon."

She frowned, studying his face, remembering in detail the steamy kisses they had shared, remembering the feel of his arms, the scent of his skin. Remembering her own potent reaction to all of that.

Panic filled her. She hauled her feet and legs into the van and shut the door. "Well, don't look at me!"

It was his turn to laugh. He rubbed a hand down over his face, pinching his chin between fingers and thumb as he regarded her, sober now. "Don't worry. I'm not. Not in that capacity."

He folded his arms on the window opening. Golden hair sprinkled his wrists and the backs of his hands, catching the sun. It dazzled her eyes, confused her thoughts. She tore her gaze away and said, "Speaking of April, where is she?"

"At Sylvia's. Eric's going to take her up for a quick flight in his Cessna after his last student this evening."

Heather wondered if Sylvia knew where Rob was. She frowned. "April's been without a mother since she was a very small child. Why the urgency now?"

"Because she needs someone now. And why wait? I simply need to find a woman I'm compatible with who's also motherly."

Heather nodded. "Motherly," she echoed, trying to envision Rob living with someone who wore aprons and sensible shoes, and had streaks of flour on her face. Trying to visualize him going to bed with some-one like that. The only picture that formed was one in which the woman lay atop the covers, still wearing her apron, sensible shoes, and the flour. Her feet were crossed at the ankles.

"After her parents were killed"—Rob spoke and Heather jerked back to attention—"April went to live with her grandmother. I thought that was as it should be, because a little girl needs a woman's influence, a stable home, and I tend to move around a lot. But when the grandmother got married and decided she didn't want April anymore except for vacations, that left me."

"And you took her, just like that. Despite moving around a lot." Despite not being a family man.

"Naturally. She's my brother's child, and we're the only two left of our immediate family, April and I." For a moment, he looked far away and lost, then he blinked and was himself again. He stood back from her van, leaning on the hood of the car parked in the next slot.

"In Germany it all worked out pretty well. I already had a housekeeper who lived next door and was more than willing to help me with April."

"And you can't get a housekeeper here?" A house-keeper fit much better the picture she had of the woman in the apron. Yes, a housekeeper was clearly the answer. Why in the world did Rob think he had to get married?

"Yes, I could, but I realized last week that a succession of housekeepers is not what's right for April."

"What brought you to that conclusion?"

He sighed as he rubbed his toe in the gravel. "She

admitted the other day that she cries for Frau Fischer in the night. She doesn't want another housekeeper that we'd have to leave behind."

Heather's eyes widened. "So you decided a wife was the answer. And Eric and Sylvia are looking for suitable . . . companions for you."

He looked at her again. "And for you."

She laughed. "They're out of their little minds, aren't they?"

"Throwing the two of us together? So it would seem." He came back to the van and leaned on the door, running his fingertips along her arm from her wrist to her elbow. She shivered delicately. "Except, he murmured, "there's this."

She snatched her hand inside and rubbed her arm vigorously. "'This,'" she said, "isn't something we're going to pursue."

He, who didn't chase women, said softly, "Isn't it?"

"No." She was adamant.

She was just as adamant in her refusal of his dinner invitation. If he hadn't stepped back, she just might have run over his toes.

Heather wished she knew why she was doing this. She clenched her teeth as she sat behind the wheel of her car, staring out the windshield at the back end of Rob's car. It wasn't too late. She could start the engine and drive away again. She didn't have to go through with it. She could go home and make her proposal over the phone.

Friday evening. She'd thought he wouldn't be home. She'd almost counted on it. But his car was parked just ahead of hers. Right outside his house.

She opened her car door and got out, disgusted with herself for the weakness of her knees. For heaven's sake! He was only a man. A man who had a problem that required a solution. A solution she was sure she could provide.

And she was a woman who could use a bit of a helping hand too. There was nothing more normal than the two of them assisting each other. Mutual aid. *Nations* did it.

She strode determinedly up the front walk and rang the bell.

Rob hadn't even recovered from his surprise of seeing her, when she blurted out what she had to say, still standing on the doorstep. "If you'll help me for the month that my parents are here"—she drew a deep breath—"then after they've gone, I'll help you find a wife."

His jaw dropped as he stepped back, letting her come in. He closed his mouth and opened it again in a rude shout of laughter. "You'll what? Lord love a duck, Heather! How appropriate do you think any of your friends would be?"

She bridled, gripping her hands together. "Hey! I have some pretty nice friends, you know. Progressive. Intelligent. Stimulating."

He smiled at her vehemence as he took her hand and drew her farther into the room. "And they all do outrageous things in their spare time, or they wouldn't be your friends."

"They do *interesting* things," she corrected him as she plopped down in the chair he gestured to. "And any one of them would make a fine wife for any man and a good mother for his children. But the two I was thinking of as immediate possibilities for you to

meet—an accountant and an electrical engineer—
have one important factor in common. They're living
with the sounds of their ticking clocks. I've heard
both of them say at one time or another, and in one
way or another, that it's getting harder and harder to
find a man to date, that all the single men in our
age-group are either taken or gay, or have serious
personality defects."

He sat back down on the couch and shut off the
baseball game on TV. "A career woman? Not a
chance." He set the remote control down with a
decisive click. "My wife is going to stay at home. Be
there for April. After all, that's what I want her for.
Someone whose mind is focused on advancing her
position in the corporate world wouldn't do."

Heather clenched her hands on the arms of the
chair. "I can't believe I'm hearing this! You'll expect
your wife to stay home all day to make tuna casse-
roles and knit mittens while watching the soaps?
You're looking for someone who'll spend her eve-
nings running up draperies and slipcovers? Women
have jobs now. Professions. Positions they've worked
hard to earn. We're not content with needlepoint."

"What's wrong with needlepoint?" He waved a
hand toward the windows where the evening sun
pounded through the glass. "And as you can see, I
haven't bought drapes yet. My mother used to sew
curtains and things. Before she got married she was
trained as a nurse, but she never complained about
staying home to take care of us and our father."

Heather made a disgusted sound. "Hell, McGee.
You're looking in the wrong era. Try time travel.
That's the only place you'll find yourself a living,
breathing doormat."

He had to protest. "You make me sound like a Neanderthal. I'm not. I'm just a man who wants a nice, quiet, well-run homelife for his niece. And I don't want a doormat. I'd hate a doormat. But I would like to meet a woman who'd ultimately come to care more about April than a career. A woman who'd be happy to stay home and be there when April comes in from school. A woman who can teach her how to be . . . feminine. Someone she can go to when things go wrong."

Heather was on her feet. "Like when she can't decide what shoes go with what dress, or her hair won't lie down in back? Someone to help her with makeup and nail polish? For that, you think she needs a mother? To giggle with over all those delight-ful, silly, *female* pursuits men find so charming and incomprehensible? You're crazy! For that, she needs a girlfriend!"

He looked up at her, frowning. "What the hell are you so incensed about? Just because I rejected the idea of meeting one of your friends?"

"Of course not. It's simply the idea of your wanting a grown woman to spend her days being a girlfriend to April."

"There'd be more to it than that, of course. But one of the problems that's cropped up right here and now is that April doesn't *have* girlfriends. This minute, she's outside riding her bike, alone, and if I hadn't forced her to go out and get some fresh air, she'd be in her room moping. She says the kids all hate her, pick on her, make fun of her, and *I* can't figure out why. She got along okay in school before we moved.

"It would help her to have an understanding woman on hand when she's got the blues, or when her feelings get hurt at school. I was thinking, too, of when she's a little older and the boy-girl stuff starts up. And zits. And her period."

Heather stared at him with blistering contempt. "Hire a nanny!"

Or another housekeeper? He remembered Eric saying he was looking for a younger edition of Frau Fischer to marry. He scowled, trying to envision a younger edition of Frau Fischer sharing his bed. It wasn't a pretty picture.

Suddenly, it was very important that Heather understand. He leaned forward on the sofa, arms on his knees, and looked at her intently. "April needs someone who can sympathize—empathize—with what it's like to be a ten-year-old girl, or a thirteen-year-old, or an eighteen-year-old. I can't give her what she needs. Loving her isn't enough, and I do love her, Heather. But I feel totally inadequate all too often because I don't know how she feels, or how to respond to her obvious needs."

He rubbed his hands over his face. "Hell, you'd think a man who's dedicated his life to healing people would have some kind of built-in ability when it comes to fathoming the inner workings of a little girl. But there are times when I simply can't understand her moods. I have friends who tell me they're only going to get worse. And they all say it with such relish, as if because they've suffered, they can't wait to see me do the same. But each one of them has a mate to share the suffering."

His jaw clenched tightly as he gazed at her in appeal. "For all that, though, it's April's suffering I want to alleviate. She's asked me for so few things these past two years. Just a puppy. And a normal home life. The one, I might be able to manage. But not the other. Not on my own."

"But Rob—"

"I only know that there are times when she hurts, and cries; and even worse, times when she hurts and doesn't cry because she knows I won't understand what's made her sad. And it makes her even sadder to know she's confusing me, worrying me. Can't you relate to that? You hate to worry your parents."

She took a rapid turn around the room. "Oh, for heaven's sake! It's not the same thing we're talking about here. I'm not actually looking for a real husband in order to make them happy."

"Maybe not, but I'm looking for a real wife."

"The kind of woman you're looking for wouldn't want you, Rob."

He shot to his feet. "What are you talking about?"

Damn the woman! She'd just put his most secret fears into words. How the hell had she picked up on that little issue? Was she a witch or something?

He strode to the window where he stood looking out, then he spun to face her. "Why wouldn't a woman want me?" he demanded. "What's wrong with me? One of those serious personality defects you mentioned? That's not why I'm still single at nearly thirty-eight. Medical school takes a helluva long time when you can't go straight through, but have to work every second year to earn the tuition for the next one. I couldn't even consider a wife! And then—"

He broke off, fighting for control. Dammit, he didn't owe her an explanation of anything! No one could get under his skin like Heather Tomasi.

"And then you joined the army to see the world," she added. "And all the women in it."

"That's right, or it was until April became my main concern." He managed a weak grin. "I may be out of practice because I haven't had much of a social life since I became a single parent, but I could pick it up again."

She gazed at him long, with disconcerting frankness. "I wouldn't have said you were out of practice."

He jammed his hands into his pockets and scowled, thinking of how quickly he'd "picked it up again" just being with her. Ah, but it came easy with her on the receiving end. Too easy, because she wasn't the one he'd be working with, trying to build something with. And this time, he thought, it would take work.

Eric had always believed it came naturally to Rob, charming women. The truth was, his success with women had nothing to do with charm: He simply, genuinely *liked* them and was always up-front about what he wanted. A woman who felt wanted felt good about herself. A woman who felt good about herself had the confidence to reach out and take what she thought she deserved from life. And if what she thought she deserved was Mrs. McGee's little boy Robbie, then who was he to say no? At least, that's the way it had been.

He continued to look at Heather. She was the kind of confident, self-assured woman he'd always been drawn to. But that was before. And she was right. He wasn't at all certain he'd be attractive to the kind of woman he needed.

"And anyway," she said, cutting in on his thoughts, "that wasn't what I meant. I'm sure you could charm any woman, friend of mine or not. But if you did, it wouldn't last. So I withdraw my offer."

Her flat statement irritated the hell out of him. Who was she to say he couldn't make a relationship last? From what he'd gathered about her, little laughing comments Eric had made now and then, Heather changed boyfriends along with the phases of the moon. And he knew she'd once been married, but no longer was. That didn't make her any kind of expert on lasting relationships, not in his books.

"Certainly it would last," he said. "I'm committed to this, Heather. When I take a wife, it's not going to be one of those 'until the courts do us part' marriages, or 'until something better comes along.' I'll be going into it with the intention of it lasting, and so will the woman, or we won't be going into it together."

She strode to within a foot of him and glared at him. "It won't last because you're looking for someone who has love to give, but you won't be offering her anything in return."

He had to back away. "What? Of course I will. I'll be offering her plenty. A man with a profession and a good income with large potential. As much as I enjoy army life, I'll get out one day and go into private practice. Probably after my next posting. I think April will need a more stable community when she's in her teens. It's rough on teenagers changing schools, leaving friends. To the woman I marry, I'll be offering a lifetime of . . . well, a lifetime. And a very loving and lovable little girl. Other children if she wants. I'd like to have more kids."

Her look of utter disdain cut him, and he twisted away from her accusing gaze.

She grabbed his arm and hauled him around to face her. "Do you think it would be enough for her, your ideal woman, to have April love her? Don't you think maybe she'd want your love too?"

He broke free of her hold, unreasoning anger burning his gut. "Dammit, give me a break, will you? Let's not rush things here! I haven't even met the woman yet and you're starting to preach moonlight and roses and . . . *love!* Lord love a duck!"

"No." She was obdurate, determined, as she planted herself smack before him. "Rob love a woman is the subject under discussion. Can he or can't he? Will he or won't he?"

"Hell!" he exploded. "You sound like one of those soaps you wouldn't deign to stay home and watch."

"It's a necessary ingredient in marriage. I don't recommend you try it without. I'm serious about this, Rob. No matter who you end up marrying, friend of mine or not, even if your prime motive is a mother for April, you'd better love that woman yourself or . . . " She flung up her hands and whirled away from him. Stalking to the other end of the sofa, she turned and glared at him. "Or you'll ruin three lives. Maybe more, if you produce those kids you claim to want."

"All right, all right," he said, sitting down again. "I know what you say is true. A woman needs to feel loved for herself. Mine will. I'll make sure of that."

"You mean you'll lie to some unsuspecting woman, just to get a competent caretaker for April? You make me sick, McGee."

"That's not what I meant! I meant, I'll learn to love her eventually. It'll come in time, when I get—" He bit the words off, shocked at what he'd almost said. *When I get over you.*

Where the hell had that come from? It was crazy. All he had to get over was lusting for her. He wasn't in love with her.

"Get what?" she asked.

He shook his head, his brows drawn too tightly together. He rubbed the deep crease with a thumb. "Nothing."

"Then why not agree to my helping you find someone?"

"I thought you'd withdrawn your offer."

She pulled in a deep breath and let it go slowly. "Oh, what the heck. I have lots of friends. Why shouldn't I help? Especially if you insist on helping me."

He tried not to sound as grudging as she had. "All right then, I guess I have no objections."

She smiled, and he stood, taking several slow steps toward her. Again he saw the watchfulness in her eyes, a cautious expression that made him think she feared him in some way.

"Okay," she said, extending a hand. "We have a deal?"

He said nothing, only looked at her, wondering what it was about him that made a confident woman like her so wary. "Deal?" she asked insistently.

Deliberately, he took another step toward her. Just as deliberately, he slid his hands around her head, into her luxurious hair, and tilted her face up toward his. As he looked into her velvety brown eyes, he heard her sigh so softly it was almost inaudible.

"Deal," he said. "Let's seal it."

Her throat worked. Her lips parted. She wet them

with the tip of her tongue. Her eyes pleaded with him to let her go. Or maybe, not to.

"I'm not grabbing, Heather." His voice vibrated with tension, with the sudden knowledge that if he'd ever needed to restrain himself, this was that time. What he wanted to do was cut loose those bonds on himself, to overwhelm her, to demand and take and conquer.

"I'm not trying to startle you. I'm doing what you told me to do." He drew in a deep breath, praying for control. "I'm . . . asking." But what, he wondered, was he asking for?

As she swayed against him, he felt the surging sob that rose up in her chest. He saw the sheen of tears that glistened in her eyes. "Rob . . . "

The door slammed open against its stop. This time, Rob didn't leap away from Heather or hide behind her. He continued to hold her as April skidded to a halt on the slippery hardwood floor, her eyes wide as she gazed at them.

"Uncle Robbie, are you *sure* Heather's not going to be your wife?"

He let his hands fall from around Heather's head and stepped back from her. Looking at her, he hesitated, frowned, then said, "No."

It wasn't until long after Heather had gone that he understood that he didn't know if he'd meant no, she wasn't going to be his wife, or no, he wasn't sure.

At that point, he didn't like the question, so he chose not to look for an answer.

He's just a man, Heather told herself over and over, as she had Friday evening. Just an ordinary man. Nothing to get excited about. And she wasn't. She wouldn't. Okay, so he had kisses that could stop a brontosaurus in its tracks, but as long as she avoided those she'd be all right. And she'd have to get used to hearing his voice, to seeing him, if they were going to work together to keep her parents happy for a month, and then work together probably even longer finding him a wife.

The brisk self talking-to was a result of having picked up the phone Wednesday evening and having heard his voice on the other end. She'd groped for a chair and sat down. Fast.

"Listen," he'd said after identifying himself— unnecessarily—"I know your parents aren't here yet, but I need a date for the Spring Ball at the officers' mess this Friday night. It's sort of to welcome me and a few other newcomers to the base. If you're not already booked up, will you come? Eric and Sylvia will be going too."

She forced herself to breathe slowly and evenly as she thought about attending a dance with Rob. She'd be in his arms, dancing with him. Music would pulse around them, through them, within them, and she remembered all too clearly what that was like. With him.

A spring ball. There'd be flowers to perfume the air. And soft lights. A warm night and stars. Just as there had been at the wedding reception. It would be wonderful. It would be . . . insane.

It would be so easy to lie and say she already had a date; he'd offered her that way out.

Maybe he was asking her only because he knew Eric and Sylvia expected it of him. Maybe he secretly hoped she wouldn't be available. That was likely why

DON'T HOLD BACK!

1. **No obligation!** No purchase necessary! Enter our Sweepstakes for a chance to win!
2. **FREE!** Get your first shipment of 6 Loveswept books *and* a lighted makeup case as a free gift.
3. **Save money!** Become a member and about once a month you get 6 books for the price of 5! Return any shipment you don't want.
4. **Be the first!** You'll always receive your Loveswept books before they are available in stores. You'll be the first to thrill to these exciting new stories.

Detach here and mail today.

WINNERS CLASSIC SWEEPSTAKES
Entry Form

YES! I want to see where passion will lead me!

Place **FREE ENTRY** Sticker Here

Place **FREE BOOKS** Sticker Here

Enter me in the sweepstakes! I have placed my FREE ENTRY sticker on the heart.

Send me six *free* Loveswept novels *and* my *free* lighted makeup case! I have placed my FREE BOOKS sticker on the heart.

Mend a broken heart. Use both stickers to get the most from this special offer!

61234

NAME _____

ADDRESS _____ APT. _____

CITY _____

STATE _____ ZIP _____

Loveswept's Heartfelt Promise to You!

There's no obligation necessary to enter the sweepstakes. There is no obligation to buy when you send for your free books and lighted makeup case. You may preview each new shipment for 15 days free. If you decide against it, simply return the shipment within 15 days and owe nothing. If you keep them, pay only $2.25 per book — a savings of 54¢ per book (plus postage, handling, and sales tax in NY and Canada.)

Prices subject to change. Orders subject to approval.
See complete sweepstakes rules at the back of this book.   CA1

Give in to love and see where passion leads you!
Enter the Winners Classic Sweepstakes and
send for your FREE lighted makeup case and
6 FREE Loveswept books today!

(See details inside.)

he'd left it until Wednesday to call her. He'd probably tried hard to find someone else and . . .

And what in *hell* was wrong with her? She was a good-looking woman and dressed up well. Enough men had told her that, so she believed it. She was fun to be with. Men *and* women had told her that. The question was not whether he wanted her to go with him: He'd already asked her, thereby making it clear that he did. The question was did she want to be with him? And the answer . . .

"We could use it as a rehearsal, so to speak," he said into her silence. "Get to know a bit more about each other so that when your parents see us together we can act like old news."

That made a surprising amount of sense she thought, but still . . . Her heart hammered much too hard, much too fast, as if she were being confronted by something mysterious and dangerous and half hidden. She didn't feel comfortable that his suggestion made so much sense.

"Uh, why don't I fix you up with a date with one of my friends instead?" she asked quickly. "That way, we could get the jump on your search."

He demurred. "Not a good idea, Heather. When I make my move on this wife business, I'm going to want to go full steam ahead with it. If you got me a date now and she turned out to be the right one, then how would I explain to her that I have to spend time with you and your family when they arrive? I mean, in the two weeks left I could get pretty well involved with the woman."

That also made sense, so she agreed to go with him.

Over his objections, she arranged for him to pick

her up at Eric and Sylvia's house, since she lived twenty miles out of town. That made good sense too. Something told her it would be a bad, bad idea for Rob to come to get her at her house. Or to bring her home after the party.

Almost as bad an idea as her attending it with him probably was.

She broke the connection without hanging up, and hit the memory for Sylvia's number. "Hi," she said when Sylvia answered, and wished she didn't sound as breathless as if she'd just swum a hundred laps. "What should I wear to the Spring Ball at the officers' mess?"

Sylvia didn't hesitate. "Your red satin, of course. Pal, you're going to knock 'em dead."

Or had Sylvia, Heather wondered half an hour later, after she'd hung up, said "You're going to knock *him* dead?"

Since that wasn't what she intended at all, maybe she should go shopping for something in gunnysack gray.

Six

Rob let out a long, slow breath as he walked across the Linds' living room toward Heather. He halted several feet short of her, and swallowed and adjusted his tie.

She wore red. He had expected that. And as red was supposed to do, it stopped him in his tracks. It also warned him of danger.

Her dress was simple, an unadorned satin sheath with spaghetti straps. It covered her full breasts decently. It nipped in at her small waist. It wasn't too tight over her hips, and it skimmed her thighs with enough room to spare, so that when she walked it didn't pull overly taut. There was nothing specific about her dress that anyone, even the most pompous of old-line officers, could object to, but he knew that the mess would be humming that night over the sexiest, deadliest garment he had ever seen. Because it was on her.

Her hair, pulled back from her face on one side,

tumbled over her left shoulder in a gleaming mass of curls. Her only jewelry, a diamond teardrop, hung from her exposed earlobe, afire with reflected light. There were rhinestone swirls across the toes of her red shoes and . . .

He blinked, then his eyes widened as he recognized the design that decorated the ankle of her left stocking; a black spider in the center of a delicate web. It didn't have the Aer-Real Adventures logo around it, but it served as a perfect reminder of Heather, upside down, swinging from her "web." He swallowed hard again and hoped his hands didn't start sweating.

She smiled at him, a tiny—and if he hadn't known better, would have said shy—smile, and lifted a diaphanous length of cloth from the back of a chair. She held it in one hand as she looked him over.

With a murmured word of greeting, he took her gauzy stole, draped it over her shoulders, offered his arm, and they walked outside without speaking further. Eric and Sylvia followed, Sylvia assuring her husband that the baby-sitter was competent, and complaining they'd be late if he didn't stop with the overload of instructions.

As Eric opened the back door of his car for her, Heather realized for the first time that the four of them would be traveling together. It was, she thought, a mercy. With Sylvia and Eric in the front seat wrangling happily, there was no need for her and Rob to try to make conversation.

She slid a sidelong glance at Rob. He stared straight ahead, his gold-trimmed uniform hat sitting square on his knees, his shoulders back, his feet planted solidly on the floor. The gold braid on his green sleeves caught a low-angled sunbeam and twinkled. His hair, gilded by the same light, was thick and so neatly combed, she ached to muss it, but didn't dare. He looked much too . . . official.

For all the attention he was paying her, she thought, she might not even have been there. Apart from his initial greeting and offering her his arm, he had ignored her.

Did he regret having invited her? Was her dress too flashy, too slinky, too . . . something, for the party they were going to? Was it the spider? She'd noticed him noticing it.

She opened her purse, took out her compact, and gave her face a quick once-over. Too much makeup? No. Of course not. In the mirror, she shot another glance at the stone-faced man on her left.

Dammit, he was doing it again, somehow making her doubt herself. It was really irritating, the way he could do that. Well, she didn't have to let it happen. She looked fine and she knew it. If he didn't like her just the way she was, tough.

She snapped her compact shut with an angry sound and jammed it back into her bag. The bag slid off her lap onto the floor, and Rob picked it up. He held it on the palm of his hand, the twinkling string of rhinestones that formed its shoulder strap draped over his thumb. To her amazement, she saw a faint tremor in his fingers. His green eyes reflected the color of his uniform, as well as ill-concealed uneasiness.

Suddenly, incredibly, she realized that he was as uncertain and as uncomfortable as she was. He, the playboy doctor, was suffering from nerves! Why? Was he afraid she'd read more into his invitation than he intended? More into the kisses they'd shared? Was he worried that he might have to find a way to ditch her when he finally met Ms. Right?

"Look at us," he said, as she took back her silver bag and placed it on her lap. "You in red and silver, me in green and gold. You'd think this was a Christmas dance instead of the Spring Ball."

"Should I . . ." She cleared her throat. "Should I have worn something frothy and pastel?"

He shook his head, his gaze warming as it slid over her. "No. You look . . . beautiful. I think I forgot to tell you that. You took my breath away."

That was too much to believe. A man like Rob would never lose control of his breathing unless he chose to. Of that, she was certain. "You look pretty good yourself. Even if your hair is too tidy."

He blinked and almost smiled. "It is?"

She almost smiled back. "I'm sure it's just the way it should be when you're all dressed up like a proper, conservative, uniformed officer and gentleman." That should remind him that she knew perfectly well why he had invited her. She flicked a quick glance at him through her lashes. "Even if it does tempt me to mess it up a little."

He grinned. "You can if you want to."

Suddenly, the evening took on a much more lustrous glow.

For both of them.

"Hi, Heather!" The air force lieutenant was a stranger to Rob. Heater introduced them as Rob got her a glass of punch. Then, another interruption. An army captain this time. "Eric, Sylvia. Nice to see you.

And you brought Heather. Great. You running another course this summer? I have a buddy who's interested."

I just bet you do, Rob thought grimly. Had he and his buddy been there for the naked jump?

Eric introduced Rob as the new base surgeon, and they moved on. Again and again, Rob was forced into awareness that he, not Heather, was the stranger here. And he'd been worried that she might be bored, not knowing anyone. Hell, she knew everyone! And everyone knew her. Why had she had so much trouble finding someone to act as a panacea for her parents' concerns?

"How's it going, Heather?" a navy type asked, resplendent in summer whites. He nodded politely to the others, but his attention was all on Heather as he asked if he could count on seeing her out there "wave skimming" again anytime soon. They both laughed, and the man chucked her under the chin. Before she could introduce him, he zigzagged away through the crowd.

"Wave skimming?" Rob slid a proprietary arm around her waist. She was his date, and people had better start realizing it.

She shrugged and smiled. "It's just a term. I don't really fly that low."

He had a mental image of her flying off the bridge and coming to a halt at what looked like inches above the deep, dark pool in the bottom of the canyon. Had the navy type been at the bungee jumping too? How many of the men in this mess had been there? He ground his back teeth together.

"Let's go find a table," he said to Eric.

They managed to get a very small one at the outer

fringe of the lounge area and, with much shuffling of chairs, squeezed all four of them around it. Heather was glad to get out of the melee for a few minutes.

Rob swung his arm across the back of her chair to give the bar steward room to set their drinks down, and when the man had gone, didn't change his position. His fingers toyed with the ends of her hair, creating little currents of electricity that trickled up and down her body, making her dress seem too warm for the occasion.

"I didn't know people took courses in bungee jumping," he said. "I thought they just went up there and dove off."

"They do. Oh, we give them instructions, naturally, tell them what to expect, but there's no course per se."

"So what's this course half the men here took from you?"

"Half the men?" She laughed. "Four, Rob. Only four. I teach ultralight flight. Two of my partners build them. I teach the customers. We fly at the private airfield where Eric teaches, and he helps me out. He gives lectures on the theory of flight."

Rob glared accusingly at his best friend. "You never told me that."

Eric shrugged. "It never came up, I guess. Last year's course is long over. This year's hasn't started."

Ultralights! Rob stared at Heather's slender arms, her fine bones, her smooth skin. His mind conjured up a picture of her at the controls of a small mosquitolike aircraft, zipping over the wave tops near a naval ship. He saw a miscalculation, a crash, those slender limbs bent to unnatural angles, that skin rent and bleeding and—

He cringed. Lord love a duck! And he'd thought it was agony watching her jump off a bridge!

Involuntarily, his hand tightened on her shoulder.

She smiled at him, kindly, he thought, as if she had read his thoughts and pitied him for being a fool. "Tell me," she said, "what exactly do you specialize in? I had no idea of your importance until I heard you being introduced as the new base surgeon. I mean, I know what an eye surgeon does, and a heart surgeon, but a *base* surgeon? Don't they merely throw old bases away when they start spilling sand out their seams?"

After the general laughter subsided, she asked, "Seriously, what does it mean, being the base surgeon?"

He forced himself to be a convivial date. What Heather did, the risks she took, were simply not his business.

"It means that, in addition to looking after troops with runny noses, I get to do a lot of administrative junk and take the flack for anything that goes wrong, from spilled bedpans to misdiagnosed hangnails."

"What? No promotion?"

"Maybe," he said. "If things go right."

"If none of your underlings misdiagnose too many hangnails?"

His chuckle was warm. "Or if I don't." He lifted her hand to his lips, brushing the backs of her fingers with them. "Do you have any that need my attention?"

Heather closed her eyes for a second, shivering deep inside at the soft touch of his mouth on her skin. When she opened them again, she found his gaze on her face, as warm as his voice had been. And filled with promises.

Promises he should be saving for April's stepmother-to-be.

Guiltily, she glanced at Eric and Sylvia, but the two of them were turned around, laughing and talking with people at an adjacent table.

Shortly after that the dinner commenced, and when that was done, the dancing.

The moment they left the dining room and returned to the lounge, they snagged a table near the dance floor. When the band opened with "The Blue Danube" waltz, Rob asked, very politely, "May I have this dance?"

"Of course." She took his hand and stood.

They walked to the floor silently. He slid his arm around her, his palm at her waist, and held her at exactly the correct distance from his body. She laid her right hand delicately across his and he held it at exactly the correct height. She placed her other hand on his shoulder, midway between his shoulder seam and his collar, and slowly they circled the floor, alone for the first moments.

As other couples joined them, he drew her closer. Their thighs brushed. Fire danced from him to her and back again. Hot, deliciously intense, dangerous fire. Exciting.

He turned her, swung her, and for a tantalizing second her breasts were pillowed against his chest, their bodies aligned from shoulder to knee, then he eased her back. Another turn, a dim corner, and he brought their clasped hands in closer. He brushed his knuckles under her chin for just a moment, as if he might kiss her, then tucked their linked hands between them. He slid his right hand up her back to where bare skin quivered under his touch.

"Lovely party, isn't it?" He spoke in formal tones.

"Most enjoyable." She drew a deep breath that was filled with his citrusy scent. Her breasts grazed his chest again. The music sobbed, whispered, and moaned.

"Dancing with you is a pleasure," he said. "You move effortlessly, like thistledown."

"It's easy to dance well to a good band," she said. She paused, glancing up at him through her lashes. "And with an excellent partner."

His mouth curved upward at one corner. His knee brushed between her thighs. Or had that been her imagination? "Did I tell you how beautiful you look tonight?"

She tossed her head back and smiled up at him as they circled slowly under the spinning overhead globe, a remnant from disco years that she was glad had never been replaced. "Thank you. You did mention it."

They spun in a few more slow, stately circles, and were in a corner.

His hand slid down over her bottom for a fraction of a second, as if it had merely slipped. His provocative eyes and teasing words said it had been no accident. "I love the feel of satin."

Her hand crept up the slope of his collar toward his neck. He drew in a harsh breath as she stroked her thumb over the skin just below his ear. "So do I."

He inserted one of his fingers just under the lowest edge of her dress's veed back. It moved in a small arc, back and forth, back and forth, between the two dimples that flanked her spine at the tops of her buttocks. "But silk is another of my favorite fabrics."

She slipped her hand up the back of his head, then let it slide down over his hair. "Mine too." And then she quickly tousled the neatly combed top.

He chuckled as his arm tightened around her and her breasts flattened on his chest. She softened, tilting her head back to look up again into his smoldering eyes. Her imagination had nothing to do with the feel of his thigh between hers. Still it went wild. His search hadn't started yet, she told herself. Not yet . . .

His hand slipped out from under hers, leaving it to lie on his chest as he slid his palm up her throat and under her chin, holding her face in position. His lips brushed hers, the tip of his tongue ran along them. The kiss was over before it really started, then he took her hand again and held it close to his body as she lowered her head to his shoulder.

For too long, she allowed herself to melt against him, barely resisting the urge to link her arms behind his neck and sway with him in one place. But that wasn't what they were there for. It wasn't why they were together.

It wasn't in the cards.

They turned again into the brighter lights, and his hand moved back into a more acceptable position. They danced three inches apart.

"Would you care for a drink?" he asked when the set was over, and she agreed.

"Why don't you look for your wife in the hospital?" she asked as, with drinks in hand, they wandered out onto the wide patio where there were tables and chairs and furled umbrellas. Tubs of flowers and shrubs stood all around. "Isn't it traditional for doctors to marry nurses? Or other doctors?"

Suddenly, she realized what she was saying: *Don't ask me to stand by and watch one of my friends take what you aren't offering me, what I'd have to refuse even if you did offer it.*

She shouldn't be feeling that way, but more and more, she did. Reluctant, angry, resentful that he'd so readily accepted her suggestion that she find him a wife. She wished she'd kept her mouth shut.

He took her elbow and bypassed the tables, going to a waist-high wall. He leaned against it while she sat on a wrought-iron bench.

"Maybe doctors and nurses are a tradition in romance novels," he said in response to her question, "but it's not one I intend to follow. I have a hard-and-fast rule about that, and now that I'm CO of the hospital it's one I'm going to have to adhere to scrupulously. No dating colleagues."

She struggled to find a solution for him, one that she wouldn't have to witness. "Surely not all the women on base are associated with the hospital. You could—"

"No." His mouth and eyes were suddenly hard, as was his tone. "We'll worry about my problems after your parents' visit."

"All right." Her voice was as curt as his. "I was merely trying to hold up my end of our agreement. My helping you find a wife doesn't necessarily mean I have to locate her within my own personal circle of friends, does it? Why not broaden the search and—"

"Dammit, will you drop the subject?" he demanded, and she snapped to her feet with a brusque "Certainly."

As she turned to march away, he caught her hand and swung her back. "I'm sorry," he said. "It's just that tonight . . ." His eyes softened. "Tonight, all I want is to have fun." He touched her cheek with one finger. "With you. Please, let's just . . . enjoy the moment."

She hesitated, too many possible scenarios floating through her mind of them enjoying "moments." For the rest of the night.

"Okay, then." She raised her glass. "To the moment." One thing she'd learned was how to control those moments and not let them get out of hand. Until Rob McGee had come on the scene, it had been easy.

He picked his glass up from the top of the wall. The gentle sound of crystal clinking together mingled with the music that had started again inside. "And to many more like them," he said.

"That's not what I had in mi—" she started, but he swept an arm around her waist and pulled her close, bending his head to hers. Quickly, she planted three fingers over his lips, stopping his kiss before it began. While she wasn't willing to admit it aloud, another moment or two in his arms wouldn't have been too far from what was on her mind.

"Uh-uh," she said chidingly, laughing. "Remember the results of a quick grab."

He let her go. "Oh, yes. Now that you mention it, I do." Taking her hand, he led her back inside. "Let's dance, Ms. Tomasi. And you can tell me how you came to have such dangerous knowledge."

"Dangerous, Major?" She set her glass on a table near the entrance and moved into his arms. Alcohol was to be avoided tonight. "Knowing how to catch an opponent by surprise and fling him flat on his back isn't dangerous. Except to the opponent."

He smiled wolfishly. "Don't be too sure that the opponent is always going to be the other guy. Maybe someday someone will catch you by surprise and you'll end up flat on your back."

This was the kind of flirtatious repartee she could deal with. She fluttered her lashes at him. "Never. Nobody ever takes me by surprise."

He laughed as the band swung into something fast and rhythmic. He spun her around so fast, she reeled and he caught her, held her for a moment, laughing into her eyes, then spun her away again.

They danced, gyrating for each other's benefit, lost in the music, the rhythm, their bodies apart but nevertheless generating a delicious electricity. Oh yes, she thought. Tonight was a time to simply let go and have fun. Other things could be taken care of later.

Such as getting serious about Rob McGee's peculiar domestic problems.

"Good night," Heather said through the open window as Rob closed the door of her car outside Sylvia's house. "Thanks, Rob. I had a good time."

"So did I. When—" He'd been going to say *When can I see you again,* but their moment was over. After a nightcap with Eric and Sylvia, they'd said good night to their friends and come outside into the flower-scented dark.

At the base of the porch stairs, he'd taken her in his arms slowly, no surprises, no unexpected moves, and she'd kissed him until his toes had curled and he was rock hard with wanting her. Then she'd smiled and backed away, heading resolutely for her car. He didn't know how a woman could kiss him until his body burned, until he knew that hers did, too, then turn and walk away as though nothing had happened at all.

But Heather could. Heather did. Heather had.

And then she'd said good night.

Instead of pleading to see her again, he said, "When do your folks arrive?"

"Two weeks from Monday. I'll call you. But not right away. They won't expect anything until the following weekend. I have a job, and they're great believers in tending to business, so they won't expect me to neglect my work to entertain them. Or my 'boyfriend' to leave his to entertain me."

He hoped his smile looked less sour than it felt. "Meaning I'm not to expect anything until the following weekend."

"You're not to expect anything even then," she said briskly, and he ached inside.

"I meant, like a phone call."

"That you'll get."

"I'll be waiting."

She nodded, murmured another good night, and drove away, much too fast for his liking. Rob knew that if he hadn't had April at home with a sitter, he'd have followed.

"It's all arranged," Heather said late Sunday morning, breathing in the aromatic steam arising from the coffee her grandmother had poured for her. "I've got somebody lined up to play the part of my boyfriend."

"Good gurrell." Margaret Campbell's voice still retained more than a touch of her Scottish accent after more than fifty years in the new world. "Tell me about him."

"He's an army doctor, a friend of Eric Lind. He and Eric have been bouncing in and out of each other's lives for years, much the way Sylvia and I have. I went to a party with him—and them—Friday night at the officers' mess in Comox. It was a lot of fun."

Margaret glanced around furtively to assure herself they were alone. "As much fun as bungee jumping?" she asked. She hadn't quite recovered from the exhilaration of her latest new experience. Since she wouldn't dream of telling her husband for fear of upsetting him, or any of her friends lest the story get out with the same result, it was only with her granddaughter that she could discuss it.

Heather laughed indulgently and helped herself to a huge square of peach upside-down cake. "Of course not, Grandy. Nothing is, is it? When do you plan to jump again?"

"Soon. Very soon," Margaret said. "After your dear mother has been and is safely gone again." She smiled impishly, her seamed face crinkling, redistributing her freckles. "How I'd love to tell her what I've done. Just to see the look on her face."

Heather laughed and leaned across the table to stroke her grandmother's hand. "Don't you dare! I, for one, wouldn't want to see the look on her face. It's going to be bad enough explaining about the ultralight course I'm starting the very week they arrive."

She shook her head. "Tell me, Grandy, how did a

high flier like you end up with such a stick-in-the-mud daughter?"

"Genetics, darling," Margaret said as Heather took another piece of cake. "Your mother takes after her father. And speaking of whom, he'd probably like some of that cake. Run and fetch him from his greenhouse before you eat it all."

Heather stood, brushed crumbs from her lap onto the grass so the birds could get them, and turned to do as she was bid. Then, spinning back, she asked, "And how did a high flier like you end up married to a stodgy old Scot like Grandpa—as much as I adore him—and stay that way for nearly sixty years?"

Margaret smiled complacently as she leaned back in her deckchair, tilting her broad-brimmed hat to shade her eyes. "Where I came from, darlin', there was nothin' but stodgy Scots to choose from, only we called them 'dour.' And as to why it's lasted, why do you think it has?"

Heather didn't reply, thinking bleakly of her own marriage, which had not.

"It's going to catch up with you one day, you know," Margaret warned.

"What is?"

Margaret laughed softly. "Love, my darling. Good, old-fashioned love. It's going to sneak up and smack you right between the peepers."

"Not me, Grandy. I'm too busy having fun to let some man tie me down again with his disapproving ways."

For an instant she recalled Rob's disapproval of her bungee jumping. He undoubtedly thought flying ultralights was as idiotic as that.

Margaret slid her hat back and gave her a steady

look from under its brim, misinterpreting the reason for Heather's clouded expression. "Gerald was the wrong one for you, love. You'd be surprised how much fun the right man can be."

"As much fun as bungee jumping?"

Margaret's laughter followed her as Heather continued on her way toward the end of the garden where the greenhouse stood. Walking slowly in the morning sun, she drew in the sweet scent of her grandfather's prize roses. She could almost believe she could hear the strains of a Strauss waltz. At once, she was thistledown again, floating on air. Heaven help her, but if her grandmother had asked her then, she'd have had to say that her evening with Rob McGee had been more fun than bungee jumping.

She danced on a cloud of memory, her arms outspread, her eyes closed, her face tilted up to the sun, and ran smack into the man she'd gone seeking.

He steadied her even as he glowered at her in vexation. "Behave yoursel', Heather. What would your parents think? Dancin' around the backyard like a wee heathen. And ye smell like a proper little whore."

Heather extricated herself from his hard, knobby hands, laughing at him. "Grandpa! That's a terrible thing to say. There's nothing inherently sinful about perfume. What would Grandy say if she heard you calling me that?"

His face twisted into a deeper scowl. "I wasna callin' ye that. I simply stated that that's what you smell like."

Heather continued to laugh as she linked her arm

through his. "And how would you know? How many have you smelled?"

"Don't be cheeky, girl. And what's the matter with the good, clean scent of soap and water?"

Heather didn't tell him that the only perfume she wore was what came from her lightly scented soap. She'd learned long ago that it was pointless to argue with him, and futile to let herself be hurt by his criticism. He had disapproved of her from the day she was born.

But that had never stopped him loving her.

"Heather has a boyfriend," Margaret said, when the three of them were seated at the patio table. "She was just starting to tell me about him when I sent her away to fetch you." She leaned forward. "Tell us both, dear. What exactly is your young man like?"

Heather leaned back, crossed her ankles, and looked as dreamy as any grandparents could hope. Though she knew this was purely for her grandfather's benefit that she was playing the charade just now, she smiled and said, "Oh, he's a wonderful man . . ."

It was a remarkably easy thing to say.

Seven

Rob still filled Heather's mind an hour later when she wandered home across the wide stretch of grassy slope and through the trees that set her cottage apart from the rest of her grandparents' property. Consciously, she refrained from dancing.

He dwelt in her mind as she showered and dressed for her afternoon out.

It hardly seemed surprising, then, to look up from the act of unlocking her car and see him getting out of his, his gaze on her face, a smile on his lips, and a bouquet of wild roses in one hand. Her heart hammered hard. Her breathing nearly stopped. Her knees grew weak, and she had to cling to the side of the car so as not to walk right into his arms. April, her face sulky, lank hair falling over her forehead in an untidy swath, sat in the car, staring at her through the open window.

"Rob!" Heather shoved her sunglasses to the top of her head. "What are you doing here?" Sylvia must have told him how to find her. Dammit, if only she could explain to her friend how difficult it was spending time with Rob. But it wasn't a difficulty Sylvia would understand. She'd say, You want the man? Go for it! Sylvia didn't think Heather's fears were valid. And maybe she was right. But what if she wasn't? Sylvia, after all, didn't know everything about Heather.

Rob laughed. "Well, hey, I've deprived you of my presence for nearly forty-eight hours. I wasn't sure you'd bear up, so I took pity on you. Now, aren't you delighted to see me? Really? And April, too, of course."

He thrust the flowers into her hand. "We stopped to look at some sea lions on an offshore rock, and picked these for you beside the road."

"I, well . . ." She set her guitar case, fat end down, on her foot, balancing it with one hand as she tried hard to think of something intelligent to say. Then she realized she should try just as hard to wipe the idiotic smile off her face. Of course she was delighted to see him—them. The sun glinted on his blond hair. It wasn't too tidy today, but she still itched to run her hand through it. He was wearing soft-looking faded jeans that molded to his body and a cream-colored polo shirt that did the same. She ached to be close to him, to breathe in his scent. Instead, she held the roses to her nose and sniffed them.

"Thank you," she said. "And yes, of course I'm glad you came. It's just that I hadn't expected to see you again until my folks are here."

The corners of his eyes crinkled with his smile. "Yeah, well, but like I said, we should spend time together. You know, make the sacrifice."

"Sacrifice," she echoed.

She nodded in what Rob took to be agreement, setting into motion a wealth of bouncing curls. He stuffed his hands into his pockets, so as not to reach out and touch. Lord, but she was a treat to look at! Dressed in white culottes, a red sleeveless blouse, and red canvas sneakers—with the laces removed— she looked about sixteen.

"But I can see that you have other plans," he said, making no attempt to hide his disappointment. "I should have called first." He would have, but he'd been too afraid she'd tell him not to come.

Increasingly, he was finding time apart from Heather was wasted. He'd developed some kind of a sickness where she was concerned, a burning inside that translated into a need simply to see her, hear her voice, touch her skin. To be with her. He'd had to come see her today the same way a salmon had to swim upstream.

Maybe if he ever got a chance to do what salmon did when they'd completed their swim, he'd get over whatever ailed him.

"April and I were out for a drive, exploring," he went on, stepping into the explanation he'd mentally rehearsed all the way there, "and we decided to stop by and see if you'd like to join us."

Heather bent down and said, "Hi, April. It's nice to see you again. Aren't you getting out?"

April got out of the car and approached slowly, eyeing Heather's guitar case.

"Is that a guitar in there?" she asked. "Do you play it?" A hint of interest colored her tone.

"Yes. It's one of my few talents." Heather laughed. "At least I think it's one. My grandfather says all I am is loud. He doesn't recognize gusto when he hears it."

"I'd like to," April said shyly. "Hear Gusto, that is. Are they a group? Do you play with them?"

Rob was grateful to Heather for not laughing.

"Maybe you'll have a chance to hear Heather play another time, honey," he said, sliding an arm around his niece's shoulders. "She's on her way out right now, though." To Heather, he added, "We won't keep you."

"I . . ." Heather looked at him, biting her lower lip as though contemplating something, then said, "I'm going to visit at an old folks' home. I go most Sundays. I wonder if maybe you'd like to come along with me, help me sing for them. What do you think, April? Do you like to sing? Would you enjoy it?"

"I don't know," April said, sliding a glance at her uncle, as if wanting to see what he thought of the idea. "Uncle Rob wants to go exploring."

Rob gave April a sharp look. Damn! Did she think she'd *had* to do this because he wanted to? The "exploring" had come about because he hated seeing her so lonely and unhappy, sitting on the front steps watching other kids play. They hadn't invited her to join them and he knew she wouldn't ask. Somehow, his car had headed, all of its own volition, toward Miracle Beach—and Heather. But since they were there . . . and since she had asked . . . He grinned at April. "Would you rather we went with Heather?"

The alacrity with which April leapt to the car and snatched open the back door was his answer. "You sit up front with Uncle Robbie, Heather. Can I hold your guitar?"

What was she doing? Heather asked herself as

HEALING TOUCH • 117

Rob pulled out of the drive and headed the way she indicated. She shouldn't be there with him. She shouldn't be encouraging either of them to think a physical attraction could go anywhere at all, because she knew that it couldn't.

Distancing. She had to try for that. Be friendly, because they'd need to be friends to comfortably spend time together when her parents were there, but she would not get involved in his life. And she would not let him invade hers.

He was going to be part of her existence for such a short time and then he'd move on, creating a life with his permanent mate. A month or two might make a nice, neat little affair for some people, but she wasn't one of them. She had a lot of dates, a lot of friends, and a lot of fun, but she drew the line at starting something she knew was destined to end.

Well, she'd started this afternoon. She'd finish it for April's sake. But then she'd break the connection.

"'Oh, don't you remember sweet Betsy from Pike . . .'" Rob grinned, listening to Heather sing. "'She crossed the great desert with her lover Ike. . . .'" Heather sang with the same gusto with which she played, with which the twenty-five elderly people joined in. Twenty-five seamed faces creased in smiles. Twenty-five right feet tapped the rhythm her guitar slammed out, and fifty hands clapped in time.

There was nothing gentle or delicate about Heather's guitar playing. She beat those strings as if trying to subdue them, and made her music lift to the ceiling, float out the open windows, and draw listeners from all over the complex. Twenty-five became thirty, forty. Staff members joined in, as did visitors.

She swept from "Sweet Betsy" into a rapid medley of other old songs, and some not so old. When she started "Puff (The Magic Dragon)" Rob was surprised to hear April join in with obvious enjoyment. And more talent then he'd ever dreamed. His niece had a great voice! And she knew all the words to "Unicorn."

"Isn't this fun, Uncle Robbie?" April asked, when Heather began a song she didn't know. She leaned on Rob, laughing up at him about a ship called the *Walloping Window Blind*, which Heather and her growing choir now rollicked through.

"I'm really glad we came," April whispered.

He hugged her tightly for a minute, wishing he could see this animation in her face all the time. He was glad they'd come too.

"Come on over here, April, and learn the chorus," Heather called. "I need your help."

Eagerly, April complied, and stayed at Heather's side until the sing-along was over.

Driving back to her home, Rob glanced quizzically at Heather. "You amaze me, Ms. Tomasi. I went to your sing-along fully expecting 'The Old Rugged Cross.' I mean, you being a minister's daughter and all."

She grinned. "I know that one too." She got the guitar out of the case on April's lap, angled it so it didn't interfere with Rob's driving, and proceeded to play and sing the hymn in her warm and husky voice. Then, at April's request, she played "Amazing Grace." Her voice, Rob thought, would do justice to love songs.

"What else do you know?" he asked quietly. "'Misty?'"

She slanted a glance at him through a fall of hair, then looked out the side window. "Yes," she said. "I do."

But she didn't play it for him.

Later, Heather wondered how it had happened so easily. She'd had no intention of spending the balance of her day with them.

But Rob had asked her if she had a barbecue, and when she admitted she did, he'd whipped the car into a supermarket parking lot and they'd trooped inside for the makings of dinner.

He'd barbecued steaks, she'd baked potatoes in the microwave and helped April make a salad. They'd eaten at the picnic table outside her kitchen, then, while Rob did the dishes, she taught April some simple chords on the guitar.

"Hello, darling," Margaret said, coming to a halt near the picnic table where Heather and April sat. Heather looked up, not surprised in the least to see her grandparents. "We heard your music, but we didn't know you had a guest." Her eyes were bright with curiosity, and Heather knew she'd hoped to find the new "boyfriend" there.

She happily stood to hug both grandparents. "This is my friend April McGee. April, my grandparents, Mr. and Mrs. Campbell. Oh, and here's April's uncle Rob—Dr. McGee."

He came out of the kitchen drying his hands on a tea towel, which he shook straight and hung neatly over the clothesline before shaking hands.

"Well, now," Peter Campbell said, looking Rob's tall, lean form up and down, then nodding in approval. "My granddaughter tells me you're a wonderful man, doctor. I've never heard her say such a thing before about a fella."

Rob smiled as he flicked a glance at Heather. "Is that so, sir? It's good to hear. May I say that I think Heather is a wonderful woman too?"

Peter was complacent. "That's as it should be. However, you'll have to look smart to keep up with her. You may think you have her hooked, but there's a real art to keeping a girl like her that way and finally reeling her in. She's a lively wee trout, is our Heather."

Rob chuckled over Heather's indignant glare. "I think I can keep up. And I'm no slouch at playing my fish and reeling her in when the time is right. And lively wee trout are more rewarding game than—"

"Listen, you two!" Heather started, but her grandmother snatched her arm and pulled her away.

"Leave them to it, darlin'. Men just have to be silly together at least once a day. If they want to talk fishing, let's you and I show April the goldfish pond." She shot a stern glance at her husband. "Maybe we'll catch ourselves a koi or two."

Heather agreed at once. It would likely be a lot better if her very discerning grandmother spent as little time as possible observing her and Rob together.

As he and Peter Campbell strolled across the lawn toward the Campbells' home and the rosebushes the old fellow was determined to show him, Rob heard a sound he'd missed for a long time—April giggling freely, sounding like the upbeat little girl she'd been two years ago. He tried in vain to see through the screen of shrubbery that separated them. He hoped they weren't really catching koi.

"Perfect!" That was Heather's voice. She clapped her hands. "You're much better than I ever was, April. Do another one."

Another what? Rob wondered. Just then the path took a turn to the left, and he saw April running barefoot across the grass, legs and arms flying, skirt swirling, as she executed a neat cartwheel.

"Heather's right, my dear," Margaret said. "You're much better than she was. Very graceful."

April looked shyly proud. "When I lived with my grandma, I went to gymnastics twice a week. I was on the novice team and we had lots of competitions." She looked wistful. "Sometimes I won prizes. I was going to go up to junior level, but then I had to go and live with Uncle Robbie and . . ." She let her voice trail off.

Her melancholy sigh reached all the way to where Rob stood with Peter, ostensibly admiring roses. He wasn't aware of anything but the revelations he was hearing from his niece.

"And what?" Heather asked after April had performed a walkover. "And you couldn't go to gymnastics anymore?" She picked up April's shoes and socks and carried them. April walked on her hands for a few yards, then executed a limber backbend. "Didn't they have gymnastics in Germany?"

"I don't know," April said, coming upright and smoothing down her skirt.

Rob frowned and moved closer. Of course they did.

On base. He knew that. But she had never asked to go. Dammit, if she'd wanted to, why hadn't she asked?

"I didn't go because . . ." April shrugged. She glanced over her shoulder and noted her uncle's proximity, then added brightly, "Because I didn't need to go. We get it sometimes at school."

Rob looked hard at April as he took several strides closer, putting himself within their circle. "But would you *like* to, April? I mean, more than just at school? Join a club or something."

Her gaze flew to his, and he swore she looked guilty. "Oh, no. No, Uncle Robbie. Honest. It's okay." Her smile was sickly, and he knew that she was lying.

"Why are you saying you don't want to, when you so obviously enjoy it?" he asked. "You were good at it. You won prizes. Didn't you like doing that?"

Her eyes took on a slightly frantic look. "I . . . yes. I mean, no. I mean . . . I don't want to go anymore, Uncle Robbie. I really don't need to."

"I know you don't need to, honey, but what I want cleared up is, do you want to?"

"No!" she all but shrieked at him. "I said no! I said I don't want to! I said— Oh, leave me alone! Why can't you just leave me alone?" She broke off, her face contorting, tears spurting. Spinning away from his reaching hand, she ran back along the path and through the trees. He leapt to follow her, then came to a grinding halt after only two paces.

"You see?" he said to Heather, spreading his hands helplessly. "Now do you understand why I need a wife? This is the kind of thing I can't deal with. The pointless tantrums followed by her freezing me out. If I go to her now, she'll turn her face to the wall and refuse to tell me what's wrong. In an hour, she'll come and quietly apologize, but she won't say anything more about it. I can't force her to talk to me. I can't help her alone. Right now, I'm the enemy."

"Of course you're not her enemy," Margaret said, patting his arm soothingly. "Heather, you go to her, dear. You're closer to being a wee girl than any of us here. Go talk to the lass."

With a troubled look at Rob, and feeling ill equipped for the task, Heather said, "I'll try. . . ."

"Clothes?" Rob stared at Heather as she joined him at her picnic table. "Clothes? I've never stinted that child on anything. She can have all the clothes she wants." He rammed a hand through his hair. "If she wanted the right things to wear for gymnastics, why didn't she tell me? Or Frau Fischer? Hell, just before we left Frau Fischer took April shopping and outfitted her completely from the skin out. She could have gotten her anything else at the same time. It didn't have to just be school clothes."

"She hates what you call her school clothes, you know," Heather said. "Doesn't she have anything else?"

He scowled. "Sure. She must have. But . . ." He rubbed the crease between his eyebrows. "Well, maybe not. When we were getting ready for Eric and Sylvia's barbecue, I asked her if she didn't have any shorts to wear, but she claimed they were too small. When I said that we'd have to go shopping, she told me she didn't like shorts very much."

"Oh, Rob." Heather's tone was gently reproachful. "For heaven's sake! Poor April. She needs different clothes, but she doesn't want to hear 'have to go shopping,' as if it's a chore you hate."

He snorted. "It is a chore I hate."

"So you sent her out with an elderly lady who has no inkling of what kids wear in the modern world. April feels ugly in those clothes, out of place. So she goes around with her head hanging down and never smiling because she's so self-conscious. She thinks all the kids tease her and make fun of her because she's dressed like a geek, and she may be right. She—"

"Geek?" he interrupted. "That's ridiculous. There's nothing wrong with her clothes. They're good, expensive things. That's what she wore to school in Germany. She had friends there. April is not a geek."

"I didn't say she was. And I'm sure everything she has is very fine quality. But . . . none of the other kids her age dress like that here, Rob. Maybe they did in her school there—you said she went to a German school, didn't you? Maybe their standards were more rigid."

He allowed that this was possible. It had been a school run by nuns. What the kids wore was almost a uniform. "So what should she have?"

"More casual things." Heather thought for a moment. She didn't actually know any ten-year-old girls, but she'd seen lots of kids around town, in the malls. "A few designer labels wouldn't hurt, and some bright neon colors teamed up with black. Some lycra with lace and big baggy tops."

"Lycra with lace?"

Heather explained further, and Rob shook his

head in disbelief. Lord! Could it be something as simple as that? he asked himself, feeling even more guilty. He noticed big girls' clothes, not little girls'. Was this the explanation for April not having made friends? For her unhappiness?

"All because she's dressed wrong?" he asked. That was something he could deal with. Something he could fix. Or have fixed. "That's *it*?"

Heather shot him down. "No. Not all of it. Oh, her clothes are a contributing factor. But she looks different, she feels different. Because she feels out of place, she has no self-confidence. Kids can sense that a mile off." Her mouth twisted in a rueful smile. "They can be awfully cruel to a girl who doesn't conform to their standards of dress."

Something in her tone, that faint note of bitterness he'd heard before, made Rob narrow his eyes. "You know about that, don't you?"

She met his gaze steadily. "Yes. And so does your niece. It's not a good feeling, Rob."

"But . . ." He was still baffled. "Why wouldn't she tell me?"

Heather bit her lip. She should not be getting involved in this, but how could she turn her back? April was a little girl out of her depth. And Rob was a man out on a limb.

"I'm not sure about any of this," she said. "I'm doing a lot of reading between the lines here. But I suspect she didn't tell you for the same reason she didn't tell you she wanted to go to gymnastics. She's afraid, deathly afraid, that if she asks for things, makes too many waves, you'll send her away."

"What?" He jerked straight on the bench, shoulders thrown back, chin elevated. "But that's stupid!

I'd never send her away. Where would she get an idea like that?"

Heather shrugged one shoulder. "Like I said, I'm not sure. I only gleaned that from a few things she let slip when she was crying. I have a hunch she's convinced herself that her grandmother 'sent her away' because she was too expensive to keep, or too demanding, or too . . . something. I don't suppose April really knows what she thinks. Most of what she's doing is feeling. Feeling scared. Feeling insecure. Feeling uncertain of her right to be loved and looked after and . . ." Her voice wobbled. "And wanted."

"Ah, hell. What am I going to do?"

"You're going to find her a mother." Heather smiled, though not particularly brightly. "Although maybe what she needs more right now is a shopping consultant."

Her attempt at lightening the atmosphere failed miserably. He started at her for a long, aching moment, then buried his face in his hands.

"Ah . . . hell!" he said again as he lurched to his feet. He walked away unsteadily and stood with his back to her, one hand braced on a tree trunk, his head hanging down. He clenched his other hand, slowly beating his thigh with it as if in pain.

Heather hurt for him as much as she hurt for the little girl who now sat in her house watching a video, pretending that she hadn't been crying almost hysterically by the time Heather had reached her. Pretending nothing was wrong. April had been doing that for two years. She'd grown very accomplished at it. It would take more than a half-hour's talk with Heather to fix it.

Still, she knew she'd been able to ease some of

April's anguish. She doubted she'd be able to do the same for Rob, but heaven help her, she had to try!

She went to him. "Rob. Robbie, don't."

He didn't move. She placed a hand in the middle of his back. "It's not your fault. If she didn't tell you, how could you know?"

"Why didn't I see it?" He spun to face her, his eyes haunted. "I knew she was hurting. I just didn't know why. Or how bad. I remember what her eyes looked like the day I had to tell her that her grandmother wanted her to stay with me permanently. She was scared, Heather. Sick with fear. I held her on my lap and hugged her tight and told her it was okay, that she and I were a family and we'd be that way forever. I thought she believed me. But all that fear festered inside her. Why didn't I know?"

Heather touched his face. "You know now. And now that you do, you can start to make it better."

He pressed her hand to his cheek. "Will you help me?"

She tugged her hand free and backed up quickly. "How?"

"You said that more than a mother, she needs a shopping consultant. Could you take her? Say next weekend? I'd ask Sylvia, but with the babies, and she and Eric trying to get their flying school operational . . ."

Heather hesitated for only a moment. "Next weekend? And make the poor little girl go to school all week dressed like a—" She clamped her mouth shut, but her eyes laughed.

"Geek," he supplied wryly.

She nodded. "Geek."

Heather thought of her two scheduled aerobics classes at the health club the next day, of the paperwork on her desk that would take her right through her lunch hour. In the afternoon the jump site at the canyon was open and she had to be there. She'd have to get the shopping done by noon so she could make that. Someone else could take the classes. And paperwork could come home with her.

It could wait. April could not.

"Are April's marks good enough that she could miss a morning of school? Say, tomorrow morning?"

Rob's smile was one of total relief. "You bet," he said, and picked her up, spinning her around and around until they were both dizzy. His laughter drew April from the house, and he set Heather down quickly.

"Movie all over, honey?" he asked. "Ready to go home?"

Heather walked them out to their car and watched them drive away. Returning to her backyard, she sat on the picnic table with her feet on the bench, picked up her guitar, and slowly, softly, note by note, picked out the melody of "Misty."

But she didn't sing the words.

An hour later Heather lay wide awake in her bed, deciding she hated crickets. Someone should invent a specific insecticide just for them so decent people could get an hour or two of sleep instead of being kept awake by that incessant chirping. Stupid bugs! She was still tossing angrily when the crickets finally shut up, but then the birds began their first-light wake-up call and she still had Rob on her mind.

What, she wondered, had possessed her to take on the task of outfitting April McGee? That was a lousy way to distance herself from April's uncle.

The next morning, however, she had to admit that shopping with April was more fun than she'd had in a long time.

April was an eager shopper, an avid one, and if Heather hadn't restrained her, she'd have ricocheted giddily from store to store. She squealed in delight over a T-shirt she saw in one window, insisted on trying it on, then wanted to dash, still wearing it and unpaid for, across the mall to try on a pair of pants and see how they'd look together.

"Can I do this?" she asked, tugging a short, bright orange skirt over a pair of pink leggings with lacy trim. She smoothed her purple cotton sweater over her flat chest. "I mean, does it look okay?"

It looked terrible. But it looked exactly the way other kids' clothes looked. Heather leaned back against the wall of the small dressing room and smiled indulgently. "Does it feel okay?"

April beamed and bounced in her new sneakers. "It feels great." She grinned conspiratorially. "Frau Fischer would hate it! She cared a lot about what went with what, what colors looked all right together. 'And children,'" she said, her eyes big and owlish as she obviously quoted, "'don't wear black unless it's to a funeral.'"

Heather patted the shopping bag that held April's new black skirt, her black and purple top, and her three pairs of jeans, one stonewashed, one regular, and one very, very black. "Well, now you can wear whatever you like."

April tugged the purple sweater off over her head and tried on a green T-shirt. "This is sort of the color of Uncle Robbie's uniform. Think he'll like it, Heather?"

"I wouldn't be surprised." The green T-shirt was the tamest thing April had tried so far, despite the long, red-beaded fringe that extended halfway to her knees. She opened the bag with the jeans. "Here, try it on with these," she suggested, handing April the stone-washed pair.

"I'd really like to have it," April said moments later, spinning and sending the strings of beads out in a swirl. They clattered against her skinny thighs as she halted.

"Then we'll take it. Want to go look at gym clothes next?"

When they were finished and on the way to school, April proudly wearing one of her new outfits, she leaned her head against Heather's shoulder. "Do you think Uncle Robbie's gonna be mad? I mean, we spent a whole lot of his money."

"Uncle Robbie is not going to be even a little bit mad. He told us to spend whatever it took, remember?" She ruffled April's hair. "You're a new woman, my friend."

"Not yet. When I get my hair cut, then I'll be a new woman. You won't forget to ask Uncle Robbie if it's okay, will you, Heather?"

"I won't forget. Now scoot. That sounds like the bell to me. Lunch hour must be over. Go on, now," she urged, giving the suddenly reluctant April a small shove toward the door of the car. "Don't be shy. And remember, ask some other girl today what her name is. Maybe she's feeling just as lost and lonely as you are."

April half opened the door, then turned back to fling herself on Heather. "I *love* you!" she said fiercely, then ran to the school.

If taking April shopping was a poor way to keep herself apart from April's uncle, Heather concluded late that afternoon, so was impulsively accepting a dinner invitation from him. When he phoned her at the office at five, though, she was just back from the canyon, tired, hot, and disgruntled, and not very quick on the uptake.

She had only stopped in to pick up the stack of paperwork to take home with her. She shouldn't even have answered the phone.

"But I want to thank you," he said urgently when she initially refused. "I owe you so much. You've changed April's life."

Heather perched on the corner of her desk, laughing. Even over the phone, his voice had the power to make her tingle. "Don't try to tell me she came home from school this afternoon with six bosom buddies and a nomination for fifth grade class president."

"Well, no, but she—" His voice cracked, and he cleared his throat roughly. "She . . . came home smiling."

Heather melted. How could she turn down a man who got all choked up over a mere smile from his niece? "And that's such a difference?"

"Yeah. A big, important one."

"Okay, then. I guess maybe you do owe me dinner."

"And more."

She shivered way down inside at the unvoiced promise lacing his deep voice. More? Whatever it was, it would be too much for her to handle. "I'll settle for dinner."

"I won't," she thought she heard him mutter, and something leapt wildly inside her.

It wasn't all fear.

Eight

She must have imagined Rob saying that he wouldn't settle for just dinner, Heather decided later that evening. Because dinner was what he settled for. That, and a very pleasant time talking, laughing, getting to know a lot more about each other.

And then, like a fool, she took what had started out like an ordinary good-night kiss between two people who were becoming good friends, and sent him running for his life.

His mouth, so firm, so warm on hers, set her on fire. In only seconds the heat built, threatening to burn her up, and her inflamed reaction ignited him. He clamped his hands under her bottom and lifted her to him, holding her, moving her against him. She whimpered from the agonizing ecstasy of feeling him grow hard, harder, needing her, and her mind shut down, letting her body take over. Letting her needs, long suppressed, surge forth.

She tangled her fingers in his hair, raked her nails

over his scalp, slid her hands down his neck, and splayed them over his shoulders. Their tongues matched thrust for thrust, advancing and retreating, dancing in a fury of sensation. With an inarticulate sound, he tore his mouth from hers and pressed it against a pulse point in her throat, as his hands slipped free the top few buttons of her blouse.

She arched into his hand, aching for his caress, and released a long, trembling sigh of pleasure when he cupped a breast in his palm. She gasped with the sharp goodness of the sensation as his finger and thumb took her nipple and squeezed, tugged. He scraped his nail over it through a layer of satin and lace, sending coiling heat to the base of her belly.

It was too much. It was not enough. His lips moved down her neck, over her collar bone, kissing, nipping, skimming the top curve of her breast, around the edge of her bra. His mouth. Oh, God, how she wanted his mouth on her. She was on fire with need. . . .

She bared her breasts for him with one quick flick of the front clasp of her bra. "Kiss me there," she whispered urgently. "Suck on me hard, Rob. Please!"

He pushed her away, running a shaking hand into his hair and staring at her as if he'd never seen her before. "No! I . . . Heather, I'm sorry, I can't. Oh, hell! What have I done?"

Nothing, she wanted to say, but misery locked the words in her throat. She leaned back on the door of the coat closet, closed her eyes, and prayed for immediate death.

He bent down, and all she felt was a gentle brushing of his lips over her cheek, a flicker of motion as his fingers passed through her hair. With another murmured apology, he left. The snick of the door closing felt like a bullet in her heart.

Half an hour later she sat at her kitchen table, the remains of a frozen chocolate cake before her. Shame swept over her in never-ending waves, along with a terrible, gnawing sense of humiliation. She knew that would cling to her like a bad odor for a long time to come.

Maybe he hadn't left because she'd been too aggressive, she told herself, but she didn't even begin to believe her own futile attempt at reassurance. Maybe, she thought, it was simply that he'd come to the same conclusion as she had, that it was best if they didn't get too close. Because where could it possibly go, with him wanting a wife?

Nowhere, she reaffirmed as she stuffed the cake wrappings into the garbage. She strode to her bedroom, kicked off her shoes, and stripped off her clothes. She rolled her pantyhose down and tugged a nightshirt over her head. Determinedly, she stomped back to the corner of the living room where she kept her desk.

As of this minute, she would stop thinking about him. She would work. Work until her brain was too tired to think.

The Goods and Services Tax report she had to file quarterly was a pain, but one that had to be endured. The only way not to have it hanging over her head was to sit down and do it. As she would have had she not taken the morning off to go shopping with April.

Or the evening to have dinner with Rob.

A sob rose up in her, but she choked it down. Dammit, why couldn't she stop thinking about him?

His face superimposed itself in front of her adding machine. She wanted to pound her head against her desk. Talk about pains that had to be endured!

Like an endless loop, their kisses and caresses replayed in her mind. And the questions. The second guessing.

Why hadn't she simply kept silent about her wants, her needs, and let him take the lead? Why had she allowed herself to get carried away like that? Why couldn't she act with him the way she had with every other man she'd dated since her divorce?

Inhibited, the more polite ones had called it. *Cold* and *frigid* were the terms Donald had used. But with Rob, she was neither. With Rob, she was like a newly awakened virgin who had just discovered what her body could do, and wanted to do it all the time.

The way she had been with Gerald.

And like Gerald, Rob had turned from her in disgust.

A simmering pressure tightened her fingers around her pencil as she entered a series of totals in her ledger. She tried to add a column of figures. Her fingers kept hitting incorrect keys, and she muttered a string of curses that would have made her mother blanch.

Disgusted with herself, she threw her pencil across the desk. It smashed against the spine of a book and rebounded straight toward her, jabbing her arm, a mute reproach against temper tantrums. She rubbed the small dark spot and cussed again.

The McGees had already caused her to waste too much of the day. She had to get hold of herself. She had to get this work finished so she could go to bed and get some much-needed sleep.

Twenty minutes later she was no closer to being done than when she'd started. She groaned, slapped her ledger shut, and stomped off to bed.

The GST could wait.

Fifteen minutes after that, she flung back her sheet and leapt out of bed. Angrily, she tugged on running shorts and a T-shirt over her too-hot skin and stormed outside. The slamming of her door momentarily stilled the crickets.

She'd run. That's what she'd do. She'd run until she was ready to drop, then she'd run all the way back home and then, by heaven, she'd be able to sleep.

She hadn't reached the end of the driveway when a car came sweeping in, its headlights dazzling her. She darted sideways onto the grass and flung an arm up to shield her eyes. The car stopped, and she dropped her arm in time to see the door swing open, bouncing on its hinges. Rob unfolded himself from behind the wheel and planted himself before her.

The side wash of the headlights turned his skin milky white and his hair silver.

"Where the hell are you going?" His whisper had all the characteristics of a shout.

"Running."

He glared at his watch, then at her. "At midnight? Why?"

"I couldn't sleep!" Her reply, meant to be calm and reasonable, emerged in a blame-filled wail.

He lifted one hand, then let it fall to his side without touching her, but his angry look softened. "Yeah. I know the feeling." His gaze swept over her as his headlights had, only with ten times the intensity. "But look at you, Heather. You're barefoot! You can't go running without shoes."

She glanced down. "So I am. I guess I forgot . . ."

He tilted her face up with one fist, gentle under her chin. "Me too," he whispered. "I forgot something too."

She looked at him for a long moment while she held her breath. Her chest hurt. Her chin and her bottom teeth ached in the strangest way. He gazed back at her as if waiting for some kind of signal. What did he want from her? Why was he there?

"What did you forget?" she asked.

"This," he said on a groan, and reached for her.

She moved into his arms as though her heart knew she belonged there. Rob held her, rocking them both from side to side as he stroked her hair, her neck, her shoulder and arm, whispering her name over and over between kisses. She was so sweet he knew he'd never get enough of her.

But he had to try. He had to ease this torture. His soul cried out with the need to join with her. She clung to him, parting her lips eagerly, and he plunged his tongue inside as he strained her closer. He lifted her against him, moving her up and down along the hardness of his sex. It was hell. It was heaven. It was intolerable, needing her like this, not taking her, when she was so willing, so yearning, so giving.

With another groan, he set her back on her feet and let her go, slowly, reluctantly, sliding his hands over her shoulders and down her arms to her elbows.

Her breathing was as unsteady as his, catching as she inhaled, trembling as she exhaled. Her palms lay flat on his chest and her eyes glimmered between her dark lashes, capturing starlight, reflecting it back at him.

"There's something wrong with your memory," she said. "You didn't forget to do that." Her voice wobbled, but she went on. "You did it, and I . . . scared you away." She laughed raggedly. "Imagine! The playboy doctor scared off by a mere woman."

He drew her close again for an instant, about all he could tolerate at that point. Otherwise he might toss her to the grass at the side of the road and fling himself on her. "Never." He set her away and looked into her eyes. "Did you want me to stay?"

For a moment, he thought she was going to deny it, then she nodded. "Yes. But—"

He traced her eyebrows with one finger. "But what?"

She moved away from him. "But it was a good thing you were sensible and left. Because if you hadn't gotten scared, I might have. I probably would have. I don't have—I haven't had—idle affairs, Rob. I was married once. It didn't work out. Since then, I've had one other serious relationship." She tilted her head back, meeting his gaze openly. "One other *sexual* relationship. It didn't work out either."

He nodded and turned back to his car, shutting off the headlights and the ignition. He hated it when she spoke of other men, and he closed the door with understated violence.

"Sometimes things don't work out," he said, walking back to her. "And sometimes they do. If both people want them to."

"Both times," she said quietly, "it was my fault."

He slid a hand into her hair, pushing it away from her face. "What makes you think that?"

"It's not simply a case of thinking it. I know it for a fact." She slipped away again, taking several steps toward the house. He caught her at the steps to her front porch, taking her hand.

"I'm not letting you walk away from this, Heather. If I can't, you can't."

She tossed her hair back and looked up at him. Even in the bright moonlight, he couldn't read her expression. "You're the one who left, Rob." He heard the hurt in her tone.

"I know. I got all the way home. I thought I was safe, thought I had made it, but—" He broke off, frowning. "I had to come back. I knew that as well as I've ever known anything. You and I are, as I said before, connected in some way.

"I lied to the baby-sitter," he went on, not quite able to believe he'd done something so base. "I told her I'd been called in to the hospital. She said there was no problem, that she was prepared to spend the night with April and get her off to school in the morning. She's a nice, grandmotherly type, and I took advantage of her. That doesn't make me feel very good about myself, but I had to do it. I had to come back here because . . ." He let his voice trail off and shook his head, frowning.

She walked up the steps, then looked down at him. "Because what?"

"Heather, may I come inside? I need to talk to you. I know it's late, but there are things I have to say to you. Please?"

Heather took a step back, coming up against the screen door, and wished she could see his face clearly. She thought if she could, she'd read in his eyes the seriousness she heard in his tone.

He was going to tell her that he wanted out of their agreement, that he had to walk away from their sexual attraction before he got embroiled with her.

His words *I thought I was safe, thought I had made it*, echoed in her head. Of course it would be best that way. She knew it too. She only wished it didn't have to hurt so much, knowing it. But it was all right. She could handle it.

"Look," he said when she continued to hesitate, "I won't touch you again if you don't want me to. But I do want to talk. I know I won't be able to sleep until I've been honest with you. About the reasons why I left. And why I came back."

She didn't reply, only turned and walked into the house. He followed, the screen door slamming shut behind him. They stood together, not touching, in the entryway. Neither spoke. Outside, the crickets started singing again.

"We'd better go and sit down," she said.

It was then Rob realized that she was crying.

"Heather!" He swept her hair back with both hands and stared at her in the dim light coming from somewhere in the house. "What's wrong? Sweetheart, what is it? Why are you crying?"

"Nothing." She looked at him defiantly through her tears. "I'm not crying."

Tenderness the like of which he had never experienced speared through him as he pressed her to him. Lord, but she could put him through a gamut of emotions. In the space of ten minutes, he'd gone from the anguish of needing her, to anger at seeing her going out running at midnight, to almost overwhelming passion when he held her in his arms. Then from somewhere had come the strength to stop, to have everything open and honest and above-board between them before he took what she offered so sweetly.

Having that followed by this soul-wrenching tenderness engendered by her tears left him feeling weak and confused and dizzy.

The trick, he decided as he wiped her face dry with his palms, must be in not attempting to steer a course through a relationship with her, but merely to go with the flow. The journey would be worth it and, like white-water rafting, an entity unto itself, requiring no specific destination.

He tilted her face up and took her mouth with his. Talking, explanations, could wait. What he needed now, what he sensed Heather needed, was concrete proof that this was right. For them. For now.

Rob meant to start it slow. He meant to keep it slow. He meant to give her all the gentle, soothing care his instincts told him she needed, but one touch of their tongues together, and everything exploded in him. He groaned and snatched her close, closer, lifted her and swung her through the doorway into a room.

He saw a small, too short couch and a couple of chairs. The light, he realized, came from her bedroom. Without hesitation he moved that way, slamming his hip into the corner of a desk. A book slithered to the floor, sending a confetti of papers fluttering across the carpet.

Heather's arms clung around his neck. Her head was tilted back, and the arch of her neck begged for his kisses.

In her bedroom he lowered her to her feet slowly, letting her slide down his body. She stared up at him. He brushed his lips over her cheeks, under her chin, down her neck, then stopped, frustrated by the neckline of her T-shirt. Pressing his hands to her buttocks, he felt her quivering need, felt her heat through the thin, stretchy fabric of her shorts. His sensitive fingers learned she wore nothing beneath them.

"I want you naked," he said raggedly, sliding his hands inside her shorts, against hot, silken skin. "I've been wanting you naked since I first saw you two years ago."

"Yes," she said.

He grasped the hem of her T-shirt and pulled it over her head in one swift tug, flinging it aside. "That's one of the things I want to be honest about with you. I want you. I don't think I can look for anybody else, wanting you so bad. I have to get over you, Heather! I must!"

"Yes," she said again.

Her breasts were bare. They gleamed in the lamp-light as they had in the sunlight, but this time . . . Ah, this time no one else could see. He moaned softly as he cupped them in his hands. Urging her to sit on the side of her bed, he bent on one knee and took a hard, dark-circled nipple into his mouth, sucking deeply, feasting on her.

Heather sobbed once, then wrapped her hands around Rob's head, holding him to her. Her body burned. She was weak, aching, wet with wanting him. She almost spoke, then clamped her mouth shut, shuddering as he moved to her other breast.

His hands encircled her waist as he laid her back.

She felt their warmth on her stomach. Her muscles contracted in a delicious shiver as he traced a line from between her breasts to the top of her shorts, then down the center seam. So quickly, she scarcely knew it had happened, he tugged her shorts away. This time, when he drew his finger down her stomach to between her thighs, there was nothing to dull the sensation, and she squeezed her eyes shut as she pressed her legs together.

"Open your eyes," he said from somewhere above her. "Look at me, Heather."

Her lids were heavy. Her lungs felt constricted. Slowly, she opened her eyes. He molded her breasts with both hands as she met his gaze. "You're so beautiful," he said, flicking her nipples with his thumbs. "So responsive to my touch. Do you like that?"

Eyes wide, her gaze fixed on his, she nodded.

"Tell me," he ordered.

"I . . . like . . . it." The words were dragged from her, through clenched teeth. Her hair tangled on the pillow as she tossed her head. "Don't . . . stop!"

He didn't, not for long, intense moments, and when he did, it was to kneel and suckle her nipples, pulling hard, then soft, then licking lightly, so lightly she thought she'd go mad needing more. His hand stroked down between her legs, parted her, fingers moving slickly over her moistness, into it. She started to speak, broke off, and he lifted his head. "What, sweetheart? Say it. Tell me."

"I *can't*!" It was a choking cry that she bit off even as it began. She stuffed a fist into her mouth, squeezing her eyes shut. Against his touch, her hips pumped and thrust. "I can't . . . do this."

"Oh, yes you can. You will. You are. Feel it, Heather. Accept it."

She cried out again, and this time, it was his name. "Robbie . . ."

He groaned and lay down beside her, gathering her close. In his arms, in the warmth of his embrace, she felt a surge of hope that maybe everything was going to be all right after all.

"I love it when you say my name that way," he said. He pulled her across his chest, kissing her along her jaw, under her ear, then took her lips in a long and deep exploration that made her head reel. A dark curtain of desire seemed to cover her, smother her. She fought her way out of it to another level, one where she could breathe, but the desire didn't diminish. It grew, eating at her defenses. Again she moaned his name.

"I love it when you say you like what I'm doing." He kissed her neck, her shoulders, the bend of her elbow. "I'd love it even more if you told me what you want."

She wanted to. She wanted to so badly. But the words remained trapped under her fear.

"Please, Heather," he murmured. "Want me as much as I want you. Let it happen. Go with the feelings."

Her hands fluttered across his shirtfront, touching buttons, edging away. Gazing warily at him, she undid a button and slid her trembling hand inside to finger one of his nipples. Flattening her palm on his chest, she closed her eyes and went still.

"Don't you want me naked too?" he asked as he paused in his sensuous attention to her earlobe.

She pulled in a long breath and squeezed her legs around his. "Yes. Oh God, *yes!*"

He turned his head so he could look up into her face. Smiling, he let his fingers play across her buttocks, over her thigh, sending shafts of heat through her body. "Then get me that way, darlin'. Please."

Her breath so rapid it sounded like sobs, she rose onto her knees and tore at his clothing. He helped, getting in her way. She slapped his hands aside, and when the job was done, she wrapped herself around him, carrying him back to the bed.

Skin to skin, hand to hand, mouth to mouth, they rode the surging currents higher, higher, and then, with supreme effort, Rob pulled back.

He knelt over her again, proudly erect, touching her intimately, his eyes dark with desire.

"You can touch me too," he said, but when she did, he jerked away almost at once. He reached for his pants and pulled a condom from his pocket, sending a scatter of more little foil packages across the bed and floor. Keeping his eyes on her, he carefully rolled the condom on, then lowered himself to her, into her, gently, slowly, with tender care.

She stared into his eyes, then squeezed her own shut again as she surged up to him, a soft, oddly sorrowful cry escaping her.

It was as he had known it would be. She was hot and tight and pulsing, and he tried to control himself, but his fingerholds on sanity crumbled. His toeholds disintegrated. He drew in a deep breath of her scent and closed his eyes, and could no more have held back then than he could have gotten up and walked away.

He thrust into her and felt her hips rise up to meet him. He pulled her tightly to him, then withdrew partway before driving within again. She whispered in his ear, soft, sibilant sounds of encouragement, guttural little moans, inarticulate phrases. Her head rolled from side to side as he pounded into her, nothing mattering but the steady rhythm that had to continue, had to reach its final end, close, so close, but not . . . yet.

Pressure built. Heat grew. The tightness spiralled higher, higher, in him, in her. He felt the deep flutters within her, turning into stronger and stronger pulses. He fought to hold on, to wait, to ride them out; he tried not to let them carry him over the edge, but he was gone. As she was gone, wild, deliciously, maddeningly frenzied. It was all he could do to hold her. She wrapped her legs high around him, lifting and twisting and writhing. Her nails raked furrows in his back. Her teeth bit into his shoulder. Blood drummed through him as she entwined herself around him. It sang loud in his ears as the tremors came faster, harder, and a shout of triumph exploded from his lungs as he spurted hard, hot, once, and once again. And then with a final effort and another shout, he thrust harder, deeper, holding it as Heather cried out sharply, spasmed again, and went limp beneath him.

He couldn't speak. He couldn't think. He couldn't move. In time, he realized he was breathing. At least his lungs still worked. He relaxed one hand, found that it was tangled in her hair, and gently extricated it. Heather didn't stir beneath him. Was she asleep? How long had they been lying there, still linked, recovering?

Carefully, he reached between them and made sure there had been no slippages, no spills, then slid out of her. She still didn't move. He eased off the bed. Her eyes remained closed, her face composed. One hand draped across the pillow above her head, the other lay quiescent at her side. Her breathing was soft and even.

It lifted her breasts and let them fall. Light and shadow played across them, and her flat belly, and her long, slender thighs. The dark triangle of her pubic hair glistened with her own moisture, and Rob felt himself beginning to harden just looking at her. So beautiful. So sweet. So giving. And she was his.

Slowly, he backed away, going into the bathroom where he disposed of the condom. He stood for several minutes washing his hands, letting the cool water play over his wrists, counseling himself not to rush her again.

He would let her sleep, let her rest, then he would love her again. And their joining would be what he'd hoped the first time would be, slow and gentle and full of all the good feelings he wanted to share with her.

At length, under control again, he returned to her bedroom.

The lamp was out.

He blinked until his eyes had adjusted, then, in the dim glow of moonlight, he saw that the bed, which had been torn apart by their frantic lovemaking, was neat. Heather lay in the center of it, the covers up to her armpits. She wore some white garment, a nightgown, he presumed, that reached her neck. Her arms, atop the blanket, were covered to the wrists. Her fists lay clenched beside her.

"Good night, Rob," she said politely.

He took another step nearer the bed. "Good night? Just like that? Good night?"

He saw the faint glitter of her eyes. At least she was looking his way. "It's been a long day," she said distantly. "I'm very tired. I put your clothes in the living room. You can see yourself out, can't you?"

He came up against the side of the bed and fumbled for the light, switching it on. They both blinked in the brightness. She lay as rigid as before, her face pale and taut, her mouth a straight line. He noticed those things only peripherally as he fought the anger and hurt that pulsed through him.

He had wanted nothing more than to slide back into the bed with her, draw her sweet, naked body into his arms, and hold her. He'd run his hands over her silky skin, breathe in her scent, and go to sleep, then wake again and love her once more in the dawn. He still wanted that.

She lay there, however, in an opaque white gown that he was sure went right to her feet, with her legs pressed tight together so she made a long, arrow-shaped figure under the covers.

In that moment, he hated her.

"What the hell is this?" he demanded. "Some kind of feminist switch on 'Slam, bam, thank you, ma'am?' What do you call it, 'Zip, whirr, thank you, sir?'"

"It's nothing like that, Rob. We both got what we wanted. I told you. I'm tired. I want to go to sleep. Please leave."

Her face had about as much expression as a mannequin's. Her voice might have been coming from a computer. He thought he saw some glimmer of emotion in her eyes, but she closed them and turned on her side. Away from him. "Turn out the light, please."

"Heather . . ." Dammit, he wasn't going to plead! But . . . he had to know. "What's wrong?"

She neither moved nor spoke, and he stood there for several minutes, frustration and anger warring with his hurt. Finally, he did as she asked. He turned out the light. And he left.

He was glad he was able to close the door very, very softly on his way out.

Nine

Anger carried Rob to his car. It kept him driving, kept him headed in the right direction—away from her.

What the hell kind of woman was she? He felt used. He felt dirty. He felt . . . Hell, he didn't know how he felt, except that he'd never felt like this before and it wasn't fun, being kicked out in such a manner, as if he had done something terrible. But she'd been with him all the way, as eager as he, as ready as he.

Their desire had been mutual. It had exploded like a supernova, taking them both by storm, and it had been more than good, more than wonderful. The tension had been building in them for days, and tonight it had come to a head.

So what the hell had gone wrong?

There was no answer. Everything had gone right. He'd satisfied her. He was sure of that. No woman could fake the kind of climax Heather had experienced. Could she? Oh, sure, he'd seen the movie with that famous scene. He, like most men he knew who'd seen it, had suffered more than just a moment of discomfort and self-doubt; had been forced to ask himself if, possibly, all women did that all the time.

But he, like every other man he'd heard talk about it, had discounted it. So an actress could do good sound effects. There was more to sexual response than that, and Heather's response had been . . . total. So again, what the hell had gone wrong between the time he'd left her bed and the time he'd come back to it.

She had gotten what she wanted from him, physical relief, and that done, she wanted nothing more?

He pulled to the side of the road and lowered his head to the steering wheel, letting the powerful hurt wash over him. There was no way to prevent it. The only thing to do was ride it out, get it out of his system the way he'd tried to get Heather out of his system by riding out the storm the two of them had created.

But had he gotten her out of his system? No. Hell no! Now that he knew how it could be between them, he wanted her as much—more—than he'd wanted her before.

She was in him, like the anger, like the hurt she had caused, an integral part of him. She had invaded him, taken root like no other woman ever had. That was what had made sex with her so special.

But . . . hadn't those feelings begun before they'd made love? Before he'd so much as kissed her?

He remembered his uncontrollable fury when the man in the canyon had made crude remarks about her. He had come closer to killing that day than he ever wanted to come again. He remembered experiencing another hot surge of anger when she'd spoken of her marriage. Something deep and elemental in him had hated hearing her say it, because it made him think of her with another man. Doing that was enough to trigger that same murderous rage, enough to turn him into a raging primitive.

And why?

Because he loved her.

"Good God almighty!" he whispered, and he knew it was some kind of a prayer. No! No, dammit! She was just a woman, like any other woman. He pounded the wheel with his fist. He'd show her. He'd show himself.

He'd been going about this whole thing all wrong. He shouldn't have done what he had, trying to get her out of his system by making love to her. He should have stayed a hundred miles away from her. What he needed was another woman. A different one to take the scent of Heather out of his nose.

What he needed now was a whole string of women, one right after the other, redheads, blondes, brunettes; short ones, tall ones, skinny ones, and delightfully plump ones with big—

Oh, hell! He wiped wet palms on his pantlegs. Women. Bring them on. Let him wallow in them, in their dozens, in their hundreds; let him breathe in their varied scents, enjoy their diverse sounds and textures and personalities. Let him hide with them from this foreign thing that had attacked his guts, that even as he fought it grew and grew and grew until there was no way to hide.

It had to be the most rapid metastasis he'd ever encountered.

He stared at the taillights of a passing cab as shock rocketed through him. *Holy . . . mackerel!* What had he done? What had he done?

The words slammed back and forth in the suddenly empty cavern of his head, then he let his arms go loose, let his shoulders slump. He allowed the sensation to fill him, spill out of him. To his surprise, it didn't feel too bad. Love.

As wrong as she was, Heather Tomasi was probably the only woman in the world he could have fallen for. He might have known it all along, when he was putting up an unprecedented battle to get this posting to British Columbia. Everyone wanted a posting to Lotus Land, he'd heard ad nauseum from the brass. Everyone didn't need it like he did, he'd argued back, citing Eric and Sylvia's proximity as a necessary ingredient in April's upbringing. He hadn't hesitated to use his poor little orphaned niece for his own ends.

Would he have fought so hard for Cold Lake, Alberta, if Eric's fighter squadron hadn't been moved back out to the coast?

Would he? Hell no!

What was it Eric had said? "You wouldn't be happy with a wife who wasn't your type."

Wife? A wife for him. A mother for April.

Unbidden came the image of Heather upside down, plunging off a bridge with jagged cliffs on either side of her, death at the whim of an elastic cord. He shuddered.

One of the jets from the nearby base took off with an ear-splitting scream, and he watched as it turned toward the mainland mountains, toward the east, where dawn slid up the pale green sky. He'd seen the battered, bruised faces of men who'd ejected from damaged planes. He'd seen the smashed corpses of those who'd ejected too late.

His mind's eye tried in vain to reject the picture of a tiny, homemade contraption skittering across the sky, falling, no chance for its pilot to jump, no way to eject. No way to do anything but die. . . .

Wearily, Rob put the car in gear, checked the mirrors, and pulled out onto the empty road.

Heather ran. This time, she wore shoes. And this time, no car came sweeping up her driveway. No cars appeared at all. She ran for a long time, and when she heard the shriek of a jet rising into the sky, she turned and ran back the way she'd come. She needed no reminders of the air base twenty miles away.

She needed no reminders of what she had done.

Shame crawled over her skin again, and she shuddered as she ran. *Fool. Fool. Fool.* Her feet beat out the rhythm of her words. Another word added itself to the chant. *Love. Love. Love.* And another. *No. No. No.*

It was true, though. She was a fool. She had fallen in love with Rob McGee, and she could say "no" to herself as often and as emphatically as she liked. Nothing was going to change it.

But that didn't mean she had to give in.

All week he left messages on her machine at home. He phoned her at work. El stacked the pink message slips on her desk. She crumpled them each time she came in and flung them in the wastebasket.

At home she fast forwarded through each message

that contained his voice, but by the time she was done, she shook like a first-time bungee jumper.

"There's nothing to be afraid of. You don't have to see him again," she promised herself.

When he stopped in at the health club on Friday, she refused to come out of the office. El relayed a message: "What about your parents?"

She didn't reply and turned on a noisy printer to block out any more words, the rattling of the doorknob, and the slamming of a heavy male fist against the panels.

An hour later, when she was finally brave enough to leave her office, she did so muttering. "What about my parents, indeed. I told him before, if they can't accept who and what I am, then they have a problem. I do not."

But she did. Oh, how she did. It simmered inside her like a volcano. Its name was Rob McGee.

"What's that?" El asked with Heather passed her in the hall. El was finished for the day, having just taken the last aerobics group. Her hair hung limp around her face, and Heather stared at it. It was an unwelcome reminder of something that events had completely put out of her mind.

She smacked her palm against her own forehead. "Oh, no!"

"No what?" El frowned. "Heather, are you all right? You've been nuts all week. It's a good thing you didn't take any of the no bouncers. You'd have killed them. What's up?"

"Nothing. I just remembered something I'd promised to do. Something I don't want to do."

El stood a little straighter, and Heather knew she was trying to hide her weariness. El was single-handedly raising two teenagers with voracious appetites. She took whatever overtime she could get. "Something I could do for you?"

Heather chewed on the inside of her lip, tempted. But no. She shook her head. "Thanks anyway. It's not job related."

El cocked her head, regarding her seriously. "Hey, I'd do it for you for love, not money, if you need help with a problem."

Heather smiled. "Thanks. I know you would. But it's okay. It's really a minor problem and I'll find a way out of it." She frowned. "Sylvia. Yeah." She dove back inside the office, flipping on the light as she did so, and reached for the phone. "Excuse me, El."

Five minutes later she hung up and buried her face in her hands. "Great," she muttered. "Thanks, pal."

"I don't think you should count on it," Rob said as he spooned mashed potatoes onto April's plate. "Heather's a busy person. Why can't I take you to one tomorrow?"

April's mouth trembled. "Because . . . she promised she'd take me to hers." She shoved her pork chop aside so it wouldn't touch her creamed corn or her mashed potato. "She promised she'd ask you if it was okay."

Rob set the salad bowl on the table with more force than necessary. "She didn't ask me." He couldn't tell April why. He couldn't tell April that Heather had refused all his calls, not answered the messages he'd left for her, and flatly refused to come out of her office to speak to him.

"Maybe she forgot," April said.

He sat down. "That's what I'm trying to tell you."

Her eyes were big and filled with hope. "I mean, forgot to ask you, Uncle Rob. She wouldn't have forgotten that she promised to take me to her very own hairdresser so I could get curls like hers. Only hers are natural." Rob knew that. "I could phone her, couldn't I? Just to see if she remembers?" She half rose.

"No!" He regretted the barked response even as it roared out, but April didn't seem to hear his apology. She sat across from him, her eyes downcast, eating her dinner as if there were no enjoyment in it.

She was half-finished when she looked up again. "You said if I really wanted to do something, Uncle Rob, I had to ask you. I really, really want to phone Heather."

Maybe Heather would take April's call, he thought, and nodded. "All right, honey. As soon as you've finished eating."

Before then the doorbell rang, and April jumped up so fast she knocked her chair over.

She snatched open the front door and let out a shriek of joy as she flung her arms around Heather.

Rob walked through the archway into the living room and stood looking at the woman he loved. She was dressed in cool, pale turquoise, her eyes unreadable, her mouth set in a firm line. He silently mourned the lack of bright red.

Heather held tightly to April's shoulders as she gazed into the eyes of the man she loved. She could do this, she told herself, and tipped her chin up half an inch. "Hello, Rob."

He couldn't speak. He could only look at her.

"I was supposed to ask if it would be all right if I took April to my hairdresser this evening for a cut. I . . . let it slip my mind. I've been busy."

"I see." Dimly, he was aware of April gazing at him with pleading eyes.

"I made the appointment Monday," Heather went on in the same toneless voice. "Would it be all right? I thought maybe a body perm would help."

He nodded. "Sure." April shrieked again and ran to her bedroom, presumably for her shoes. He admired her presence of mind. If Heather had asked him to go somewhere with her, he wouldn't have waited for anything.

She wasn't asking, though. She continued to look at him as if he were made of cardboard and she had to pretend for some unseen audience that she was speaking to a real man. She wasn't as good an actress as she was a singer.

But again, he had to wonder if maybe she'd learned something from watching Meg Ryan do her famous restaurant scene.

"We discussed it when we were buying her clothes Monday morning. Is she still happy with them?"

Rob jerked himself back to attention. "Oh, yes. She seems to be. She was sure you wouldn't forget. About her hair."

"I nearly did. I—" She broke off, obviously relieved when April came out, a smear of toothpaste on her chin and her hair more or less brushed. She wore a pair of red, pink, and yellow canvas shoes. With the laces removed.

She slipped her hand into Heather's and smiled happily. "I'm all ready. Did Uncle Robbie give you the money?"

"This is my treat," Heather said, then hustled April out of the house fast.

But Rob had made no effort to follow.

Heather wandered up and down the mall while April's hair was being done. She looked into her favorite children's store and picked up a pair of T-shirts for the twins. In a boutique, she fingered a peach-colored satin teddy.

I love the feel of satin. . . . A Strauss waltz and a husky voice echoed in her mind. Other sensations rippled through her body. She put the teddy back.

In the supermarket she bought a selection of Twinkies and a bag of marshmallows. She was almost at the checkout when she went back and dove into the Sara Lee section of the frozen-food aisle. By the time April was ready to leave, the two of them, and the hairdresser, had demolished the marshmallows.

"I love it." April pulled the visor down for the third time and beamed at her reflection. Her once-lank hair curled around her head in a bouncy halo. She opened the bag on her lap and took out her can of mousse, shaking it vigorously. "Is this what you use to make your curls stay in, Heather? When mine gets long, will it look just like yours? When I'm a teenager, maybe I'll dye it black. Or red like Sylvia's sister, Jasmine. Did you know Sylvia has a sister with hair exactly the same color as Magda's coat?" She sighed gustily. "Magda's puppies are ready to leave her now. And Uncle Robbie still doesn't have a wife to stay home and look after my dog in the daytime. I don't know when he's going to find one. Do you think she'll like my hair?"

April chattered all the way back to her house, scarcely noticing that Heather replied distractedly when at all. She was too thrilled with her new look to think about anything else.

"Uncle Robbie's car's gone," she said as Heather pulled to a halt outside the house. "Mrs. Canso's here."

"Maybe he's out looking for his future wife," Heather said, not meaning to sound so biting.

April frowned at her. "But where? The only ladies he knows are you and Sylvia. No. He must have gone to the hospital." She got out of the car and scuffed her way up the walk, Heather following. "I wanted him to see my hair before I slept on it."

Heather was sorry she'd teased April. To her, Uncle Robbie's wife was serious business. To him, as well. "It's okay, hon. Your hair's still going to look pretty in the morning. And remember what Becka said—as soon as you wash it, it'll curl up tight again."

A strange woman opened the door. She beamed at April, to whom she obviously wasn't strange.

"See, Mrs. Canso? See my hair? Do you like it?"

"Oh, I do! Aren't you something! Very, very pretty, April. And is this your friend Heather? Come in, come in. I'm Sheila Canso. Dr. McGee was called out. Would you like to wait for him? May I offer you some coffee? I know he'll want to thank you himself for your kindness. He may be back any time."

"No, thank you," Heather said. It was hard to respond normally. "I won't wait." *He went out so he wouldn't have to see me.* She fluffed April's curls and made a quick departure.

Heather juggled bags as she wearily climbed out of her car. She dropped the one with the babies' T-shirts as she fumbled for her house key. As she opened the door, she kicked the bag inside. It came to a stop against a large running shoe.

Everything—her heart, her lungs, her brain—came to a dead stop. She didn't look up.

He took the supermarket bag from her. She bent and picked up the fallen one.

"Your grandmother let me in."

Heather nodded and finally looked at him. "My grandmother likes to think she knows what's best for me."

He stepped back into the living room, making room for her to leave the entry. "You don't agree."

Heather pitched the bag of baby clothes onto a chair. "That's right."

She took the groceries from him, heading for the kitchen. He followed. She unloaded the bag, and he did an inventory as he took the items off the counter and stuffed them into the freezer.

"Two chocolate cakes. A chocolate cream pie. Mmm, banana bread. Hostess cupcakes."

"Leave those out."

He not only left them out, he opened the first package for her. She pulled out a chair and sat down.

"Would you like one?"

He shook his head, straddling a chair opposite her, leaning his arms on the back. "I don't need one."

She swallowed, licked crumbs and icing off her lips, and said, "Neither do I. I simply . . . like them."

"No. You need them." He smiled. "Endorphins."

She was silent. She knew what endorphins were.

He reached across the table and stroked the back of her hand. She curled her fingers into a fist. "There's a substitute for sweets," he said. "Makes you feel almost as good inside."

She shuddered and lowered her head.

"We have to talk about it, Heather."

She nodded. "We could go for a walk."

Rob picked up a flat stone and skipped it across the lightly rippled surface of the bay. Overhead, a flock of geese headed inland for the night. A lone gull wheeled and skimmed the water, picked up something small and shining, then dropped it and swooped again.

"I got married when I was seventeen."

He didn't look at Heather, just selected several more rocks and sent them bouncing across the water. Nor did he answer. He simply waited for her to go on.

"He was a very nice man. My parents liked him a lot. He belonged to our church. He was forty."

The next rock, ready for tossing, bit into his flesh as he clenched his hand.

"I was finished with school and had gone to spend the summer with them before starting college. Gerald was a lay minister who had gone to help them during his vacation. My parents were very happy that he wanted to marry me. I think they were glad to have me off their hands, out of their hair. And I know they worried, thinking about an innocent like me in the wicked atmosphere of college. Married, of course, I'd no longer be their concern."

Rob let the rock fly. It missed the water entirely, ricocheting off a larger rock and tumbling to the beach in a shower of barnacle shells. He and Heather walked on in silence for several minutes. "So you got married."

"Yes. My reasons seemed sound at the time. Aside from some tremendous parental pressure, I was nervous myself about attending college, going off alone. Marrying Gerald seemed much safer, and even more exciting."

She laughed and shook her head, as if at her own naïveté. "As for Gerald . . . The poor man. He thought he was getting an innocent, virginal little bride. He was right, of course. I was a virgin, and coming right out of the kind of boarding school I'd spent the previous eleven years in, I was very, very innocent. I wasn't even absolutely sure of what would happen on my wedding night. I had a fair notion of the mechanics of it, of course. Not even my school could prevent that, though they did try. And smuggled-in books had suggested that it might hurt some.

"But Gerald was the one who really suffered. He simply wasn't prepared for what he unleashed on our wedding night."

She laughed again. "It was really quite funny, I guess. Looking back on it, I do see that. But at the time, it was . . . confusing, to say the least. I was so scared to start with, then when I discovered all those delicious physical feelings a man and a woman could create together, I never wanted to stop. My, uh, enthusiasm triggered something in Gerald that I guess he hadn't . . . known before and we . . . well, we were extremely compatible. In bed. Even the first time. It didn't hurt."

Rob clenched his teeth so tightly his jaw ached. His blunt nails dug into his palms. He waited out Heather's brief silence, listening to their footsteps crunching in broken shell.

"When it was over," she said, a faint wobble in her voice, "Gerald was appalled. He got up and prayed for our salvation. He explained to me that what had happened to us—between us—was wrong. Oh, it was right that we had made love. We were husband and wife. It was my duty to submit to him, to be a vessel for his seed. Those were his words. But neither of us should have succumbed to carnality. He said God had made man and woman capable of copulation for the purpose of procreation, not bodily pleasure, and since we had taken too much pleasure from it, we had to . . . atone."

Her steps quickened. "Gerald prayed very . . . loudly, asking God's forgiveness. I remember sitting on the bed looking at him as he knelt on the floor, and I was horrified. Not only was I seeing a side of him I'd never even guessed existed—despite his missionary work—I couldn't understand what I'd done wrong." She bent back a tree branch growing out over the beach and snipped a leaf from it, twirling it between her fingers as she strode on. "Gerald prayed for a long time that first night. And every night thereafter for nearly a year."

She stared straight ahead, concentrating on walking the length of a log at the top of the beach. She jumped off the other end and continued. "I knew he didn't want to make love to me. He did it because he couldn't help himself. He said there was a devil in me." She crumpled the leaf and let it fall. "He said that I was bad.

"Because of my innate badness, he wouldn't let me go out alone. I couldn't have friends. I couldn't have a job. I had to stay at home and be a good wife. Keep his house. Make his meals. Launder his clothes." Her breath came in quick spurts. "And to be there whenever the 'devil' in me forced the 'devil' in him to knuckle under. Day or night."

"Heather, please don't. I get the picture. You don't have to continue."

She brushed off his hand. "He owned a hardware store in Winnipeg. We lived in an apartment above it." Another breathy laugh escaped her. "Those devils got together pretty often that first year.

"That sort of became a routine. We'd go to bed, make love while he shouted at me and called me a temptress, a siren, an Eve. Each time it was over, he'd beg God to forgive me for what I had done, because I was only a child in a woman's form. He'd tell God I wasn't responsible for the things I did, the things I said, the things I asked for and made Gerald do. He—"

Rob's left foot slipped in the deep, soft sand and he reached out a hand to her shoulder, steadying himself. "Heather, stop it. I don't want to hear this."

She wrenched free of him and went on as if he hadn't spoken. "He made me get my hair cut short like a boy's. I had to wear dark clothes. Dark, concealing clothes. I hated it, but it seemed to help. Sometimes he'd leave me alone for weeks at a time. He said that our childlessness was a punishment for our carnal behavior, and until we learned to control that, God would withhold a child from us. But he'd succumb every so often. Despite himself.

"He called me terrible things then. He made me pray out loud with him and tell God that I wanted to be cleansed of my wickedness." Her laughter rose, sharp and high. "You should have seen us. Rutting like animals—that's what he called it—followed by all that loud, agonized prayer. It was hysterical. You could have made a movie out of us. It was—" She broke off abruptly and walked faster, her arms swinging hard.

"He would finish his prayers," she went on in a conversational tone that chilled Rob, "then scrub himself until he was nearly bleeding and make me do the same. I came to dread those times he'd come to me."

Her words tumbled out faster as her feet picked up speed. "I learned not to respond. Not to say anything. I didn't move. I didn't, after a time, feel, but still he blamed me. For what we'd done. He shouted at me. He hated me. And he screamed out those awful, vile, obscene prayers over me and . . . I wanted . . . to die!"

"Heather! Stop!" He snatched her into his arms and held her while the storm raged, her body shuddering. When it was over, he took her hand and walked slowly back along the shore, not speaking. They sat on a log near the path that led back up from the beach, and he turned to her.

The silver of the night-lit water reflected in her eyes. He touched her face, his thumb stroking the dampness from under her eyes. She leaned into his hand.

"I divorced him when I was twenty-one," she continued as if there had never been a break. "Went to college. That's where I met Sylvia. In a martial arts class. We were partnered for karate. I double-dated with her after a bit, and later, sometimes dated on my own. But the lessons I'd learned about not responding had gone deep. My mind wouldn't release my body even when I wanted it to. Guys don't like that in a woman.

"But there were other things I could do to burn up my energy."

He gave her a crooked smile. "Rock climbing. Sky diving. Martial arts. Flying ultralights. Bungee jumping. Parasailing. Driving solo to Tierra del Fuego. Running with the bulls."

She smiled. "I've never even been to Pamplona. I don't think the Spaniards let women run with the bulls."

"But if they did?"

"I might have tried it."

"Sublimation, or death wish?"

Heather turned away, not wanting to look at him. She knew he didn't mean for her to take that question lightly, as offhand as his tone had been.

"Then? I don't know," she said finally, honestly. "But now, sublimation, I suppose. I certainly don't want to die now. I enjoy my life. I value it."

"Then why do you risk it every—" He clamped his mouth shut. "Never mind. Go on."

Sifting a handful of sand through her fingers, she did. "There's not much more to tell. That's the way it was with me for a long time, until I met a man who, from ten paces, made me feel all of those things I had felt with Gerald in the early days. He looked at me, and I tingled all over. He spoke to me, and something broke loose inside. He touched me and I thought that maybe, at last, I was all right, that I could enjoy a full relationship with a man again."

After a long moment he asked, reluctantly, she thought, "What happened?"

She spilled the sand from her left hand to her right and turned to face him, meeting his gaze steadily. "He went back to Germany before we had a chance to discover what it was all about."

His chest rose as he drew in a deep breath. "And . . . were you? All right, I mean?"

She shook her head. "No." It was the faintest of whispers. "I met another man a few months after that. I thought I loved him." Her throat worked as she swallowed. She heard it make an odd grating sound.

She wanted to say that that was before she knew what love really was, before Rob had become such a big part of her life, but how could she? She couldn't just up and tell him that she'd fallen in love with him, that his actions had hurt her far, far more than even Gerald's had. If he knew, he'd surely walk away. He didn't want love from her.

"What happened?" Rob asked, and his voice held such tenderness her heart leapt. For a moment, she wondered if maybe . . .

"I couldn't make love with him," she said. "I froze up. I felt bad. I felt . . . sinful. So he left me. I understand that, of course. No man wants a woman who . . . can't be normal."

Rob slid his hands into her hair. When she was old and wrinkled, Heather thought, she'd still be able to call up the sensation of Rob McGee's hands sliding through her hair. "You can be normal," he murmured. "You are normal."

She wrapped her fingers around his wrists, loving him so hard she wanted to cry again. "I know."

"Heather. I want you."

She nodded. "I know that too. When we were making love, you said it just the way Gerald used to. As if the words were being torn from you and it hurt as much as having your fingernails pulled out.

"And then you got up," she went on. "When we were done, you left me. You got up and went to the bathroom and washed." Her voice broke. "And washed." She wished she could hold back the words, the heartbreak they conveyed. But they, like the tears and the story, had to come out. "Like you were washing me away . . ."

Ten

Rob bowed his head against her shoulder. So that was it, he thought. Something as simple as that. Only to Heather, with her history, it wasn't simple. It wasn't nothing. For several minutes he was completely unable to speak, then he raised his head and met her gaze.

He knew he had to face up to what he'd done to her. He'd done it inadvertently, but that didn't lessen the damage. Yet, looking into her candid eyes, seeing her need for reassurance, he didn't know what to say. He didn't know any of the right moves anymore.

He got up, walked away. He knew only that he loved her, that somehow he had to make it all right between them.

Returning to her, he knelt in the sand by her feet. He held her hand, feeling the chill in the tips of her fingers. He covered them with his other hand. "I don't remember saying anything while we were making love. I only remember that it was the most fulfilling experience of my life, and I wanted to repeat it much too soon for you.

"I could tell that it had been a long time for you, Heather. I didn't want to rush you, hurt you. I wanted to let you rest. I wasn't washing you off me, sweetheart. I wasn't even fully aware that I'd left the water running. I was just standing there wanting you again." He put his hands around her waist and drew her down to the sand with him, pulling her tightly against him. "And telling myself I had to wait."

She leaned against him. A faint tremor shook the hand that she rested against his jaw. "You don't have to wait . . . now," she said, but he still saw doubts in her face.

"Believe me, love." He turned his head to plant a kiss on her palm. "Please believe me. I wanted you then and I want you now." He felt her shudder as she brushed her thumb across his lower lip.

"I want you, too, Rob."

"I'm here. Take me."

She laughed, and he thought he detected a hint of tears behind her laughter. He understood those tears now, and the ones she'd denied after their first kiss. They were tears of relief, of joy in her own normalcy.

"Not here," she said, extricating herself from his embrace. She stood and pulled him to his feet. "I have a very lonely bed in my house. There's room in it for two."

He nuzzled her neck. "We're only going to need room for one."

He loved her slow and sweet, and shared with her all the emotions only she could make him feel, and then they slept. She curled warm and naked in his arms. He awoke with the dawn and loved her again as the pearly light washed over her.

"I wish I could stay," he said as they stood in the shower together.

She ran her hand up his glistening chest. "I know. But you can't. I'm taking one of Tom's new ultralights up for a test flight and you should be home before April and Mrs. Canso wake up."

He didn't want to think about her out there buzzing around the flying club's private strip in an airborne lawn chair. "April will think I'm at the hospital. I, uh, gave them your number. In case Mrs. Canso needed me and called me there. Or in case my staff needed me. Do you mind?"

Heather shook her head and tangled her fingers in his chest hair. She loved the way they curled around her fingers, clinging, as if even that part of him wanted to hold her tightly. Was that the same sensation he got when he ran his hands into her hair? Oh, heavens, but she wanted to hold him, wanted their time together never to end. But it would. It must.

It had.

"April," she said to remind them both of what was important. "She'll be awake early, Rob. She's eager to show you her new hairdo."

Reluctantly, he nodded. She turned off the water.

Heather thought it should make her uncomfortable, sharing the bathroom with him, having him dry her back while he watched her reflection emerge as the steam faded from the mirror. It didn't. It made her feel warm and safe and cherished. Part of something good.

But what was that something?

In the bedroom he pulled on his pants and zipped them, as casually as if he had dressed in front of a woman a hundred times. He likely had. He likely would again. "May I come back tonight?" he asked.

She finished drying herself and padded into her bedroom to tug on panties, and a pair of shorts.

Rob poked his head out the neck of his T-shirt. "Heather?"

She didn't look at him as she unrolled one of his sleeves, which had curled up over his bicep. "It's not a good idea," she said carefully, keeping her tone level. "It would mean lying to April."

He lifted her chin, to see her face. The towel she'd wrapped around her head slipped free, sending a tumble of wet black curls over her shoulders. A bead of water trickled over her right breast.

"You're saying no."

She sighed. "I'm saying no."

"Why don't you want me to come back tonight?"

Her gaze searched his. "Rob, I told you. I don't do affairs."

He frowned and let her go. "You haven't had any affairs since your divorce because you weren't . . ." He gnawed his lower lip and failed to continue, only watching her while she hooked her bra.

"Because I wasn't sexually responsive," she filled in for him.

He made an impatient sound, but nodded. "But you are responsive, Heather. You know that now. With me, you have no problem." Rob couldn't help the surge of masculine pride that filled him. Almost angrily, he pulled her into his arms, holding her tightly. "We're so good together. Perfect."

"Yes," she agreed, but slipped out of his embrace. He knew she wasn't agreeing to his returning that night. Or any other night.

His temper flared. How could she be so cool about this? So calm? Something important was about to escape them. "Dammit, you can't just throw away what we have!"

She flung her shoulders back and faced him down. "Why not? What do we have, Rob? Nothing that we wouldn't have to end soon anyway. Or were you thinking of carrying on our relationship on the sly after you've found yourself a wife?"

Oh, hell! That. He stared at her, jolted by her reminder. What did she think he was? What did she want him to say? His throat tightened. He tried to speak. No words emerged. He swallowed and tried again.

"I don't want a damned wife!" The words came out on a roar of despair. "I want you! You, Heather. Death wish and all!" He snatched at her arm and swung her toward him, then heard a stunned and abrupt "Oof!" force its way out of his lungs as his back smacked into the mattress of her bed. The ceiling reeled slowly over his head.

"Lock the door on your way out," she said.

She picked up a small tote, slung it over her shoulder, and was gone.

"I want you," Rob repeated, staring at the empty doorway. "You."

Slowly, a grin spread over his face. He flung his hands up over his head and clasped the headboard. "I love you, you crazy woman. And dammit, Heather Tomasi, I'm going to have you. One way or another, lady, you are mine!"

• • •

What did you expect, you idiot?

Heather wrenched the controls too violently, sending her little ultralight plane into an unexpected slide-slip. She righted it quickly. What *had* she expected, that Rob was going to drop to his knees and beg her to marry him? She knew better. He'd been up-front and clear about one thing from the very beginning: He did want a wife, but not one who worked or took risks. And in case she was under some illusions brought on by two nights of superb lovemaking, he had restated his case that morning.

When she had all but begged him to ask her.

She groaned.

When would she learn? The man did not want to get married. But he said he had to.

And since he had to, why *wasn't* he asking her? Beyond any doubt, she knew he wanted her. "Why not me?" she asked aloud.

"What was that?" Eric's voice crackled in her ears.

"Nothing. Talking to myself."

"Well, don't. I'm trying to monitor too many radios as it . . ." His voice was drowned out by the ferocious barking of a dog. "Magda, knock it off. Maybe you better head out over the salt chuck, kid. There's a lot of traffic here this morning."

There was always a lot of traffic at their small airstrip on a summer Saturday.

"Roger." Heather banked into a slow, easy turn and clicked off her talk button.

"And he doesn't just want me," she said. "That man loves me."

She knew it in the deepest levels of her soul.

Remembering the tenderness of his touch, the adoring expression in his eyes, the tremor in his voice when he said her name, she knew he loved her. A solid, unchangeable conviction that this was one thing she could count on flooded her. She laughed. Oh, yes. He loved her, and she loved him, and nothing was going to change that.

She banked into a turn around the tip of Cape Lazo, buzzed by a ferry pulling out of the Little River slip, and circled back inland, thinking furiously.

What if he hadn't asked her to marry him because he thought she'd refuse? She'd been just as up-front and clear about what she didn't want. No staying home to bake cookies and sew drapes. No minding the dog. No soap operas, no needlepoint. She'd let him know, all right, from the very beginning, that settling down was the furthest thing from her mind. As it was. As it had been.

Until she'd fallen in love with Rob McGee.

What if he thought he couldn't tell her he loved her, because she'd accused him of planning to pretend to love a woman simply to gain a mother for April? He wasn't stupid. He knew that compromises would and could be made. He didn't need a puppysitter. He didn't need to marry a housekeeper. Those were minor problems that could be solved with a little ingenuity.

What if she went through the rest of her life without him just because both of them were afraid to speak up?

A shiver of yearning passed through her. But what, on the other hand, if this was her destiny, to love men who wanted her, but who would obviously be better off with a different type?

Destiny? she thought. What the hell did destiny have to do with her? Did she have to let herself become a victim of fate? No way! And if she was the wrong type, what was the matter with making herself into the right type? Or telling him he had a screw loose and that the type he was looking for was the wrong one?

Once April had said, "She doesn't get to ask him, Sylvia. He has to ask her."

Heather laughed aloud as she flung the little aircraft into a sharp turn.

Boy, did she have a thing or two to teach that little girl! About growing up. About being a woman. About asking for what you need.

She approached the strip, dropping toward the ground. The grass came up fast, a blur, and she saw a dog run onto the strip, ears flapping, tail streaming, red coat gleaming in the sun. Magda! With Sylvia right behind, shouting at the animal. She was going to hit them!

Heather hauled back. Her plane stalled, dipped, tried to lift, and lost it. The ground was there again, bouncing her wheels up, first one side, then the other. A wingtip caught, and the little plane cartwheeled as neatly and as gracefully as ever April had. Then everything went still.

"Heather! Oh, heavens, Heather, say something! Tell me you're all right. Lord, don't be dead. I'm too young to die. I have babies to raise. If you're dead, then I'm dead and—"

"Get the hell out of my way! Let me go. Dammit, Eric, I'm a doctor!"

"You're a madman! Don't touch her! You'll grab her or something stupid and break her spine if it's not already broken. Sylvia I'm going to shoot that dog, so help me, if she doesn't stay off the strip and—"

Heather shoved a broken strut out of her way, dragged her helmet off her head, undid her harness, and stood up.

"Would you all please quit yelling? I have a bit of a headache."

They did. Eric let go of Rob, whom he'd held in a stranglehold. Sylvia let go of Magda, who sprang forward to lick Heather half to death. They stared at her.

Rob spoke first. "Are you hurt?" His voice was hushed, restrained.

She flexed her arms, bent her knees, turned her head from side to side, then rubbed Magda's floppy ears. "Do I look hurt?"

Rob's eyes burned into hers. "No. Is your spine broken?"

She gaped at him. "Are you crazy?"

"Yes, dammit! Eric's right. I'm going to grab you. I don't care if you're ready for it or not. I don't care if you like it or not. I don't care if you throw me into Georgia Strait. I'm grabbing you, and once I've got hold of you, I'm never—"

Rob looked up at the sky wheeling above him. He looked up at the woman sitting astride him. Lifting his hands, he cradled her face, inching his fingers into her hair. "Never letting you go," he finished.

He closed his eyes for a moment, then looked at her again. "Heather, I love you."

She smiled. "I know. It just occurred to me ten minutes ago that you do. That you had to. That's why I came back in such a rush. I have things to tell you. Maybe you don't want a wife, Rob, but you do want me. And I love you too. And I need you, so you're going to have to marry me because my parents would never survive my having an affair."

He grinned and pulled her down several more inches. "Are you asking?"

She shook her head, and her hair fell forward until it formed a private bower for them. "Nope. I'm telling."

"What'll you use to persuade me if I refuse?"

She brushed her lips over his. "Martial arts?" He splayed his hand over the back of her head and kissed her until they were both dizzy. "Or maybe I'll hang you upside down over the edge of a bridge?"

He smiled. "Haven't you?"

"Not yet. Rob, you haven't said yes."

"Do I have to?"

For a moment, her chin trembled. "Are you refusing?"

He rolled with her, until her back was on the ground. He placed a hand on her middle and pinned her there. She remembered that he'd once told her "someone" would take her by surprise and get her flat on her back. She'd said no, that nobody ever surprised her.

Not even his next words surprised her. "I'll marry you, Heather. On one condition."

She looked with regret at the wreckage of Tom's plane. She gave a moment's thought to the bridge and the bungees and flying free through the air, the thrill of being weightless if only for a moment. She remembered Rob saying, "I want you. Death wish and all."

She looked into his eyes and knew that with him

she'd find all the adventure she'd ever craved. And something else besides. "Name it," she said. "It's yours."

He sat up and pulled her up beside him. "Sing 'Misty' for me."

With a startled shout of laughter, she began. Two minutes later, she finished in a half-whisper that got into Rob's soul and lived there. . . .

". . . and so much in love."

THE EDITOR'S CORNER

Next month LOVESWEPT presents an Easter parade of six fabulous romances. Not even April showers can douse the terrific mood you'll be in after reading each and every one of these treasures.

The hero of Susan Connell's new LOVESWEPT, #606, is truly **SOME KIND OF WONDERFUL.** As mysterious and exciting as the Greek islands he calls home, Alex Stoner is like a gorgeous god whose mouth promises pagan pleasures. He's also a cool businessman who never lets a woman get close. But prim and proper Sandy Patterson, widow of his college roommate, is unlike any he's ever known, and he sets out to make her ache for his own brand of passion. Susan takes you on a roller coaster of emotion with this romance.

Kay Hooper continues her MEN OF MYSTERIES PAST series with **HUNTING THE WOLFE,** LOVESWEPT #607. Security expert Wolfe Nickerson appeared in the first book in the series, **THE TOUCH OF MAX,** LOVESWEPT #595, and in this new novel, he almost finds himself bested by a pint-sized computer programmer. Storm Tremaine blows into his life like a force of nature, promising him the chase of his life . . . and hinting she's fast enough to catch him! When he surrenders to her womanly charms, he doesn't know that Storm holds a secret . . . a secret that could forever destroy his trust. Kay is at her best with this terrific love story.

BREATHLESS, LOVESWEPT #608 by Diane Pershing, is how Hollis Blake feels when Tony Stellini walks into her gift shop. The tall, dark, and sensuous lawyer makes the air sizzle with his wildfire energy, and for the first time Hollis longs to taste every pleasure she's never had, pursue all the dreams she's been denied. Her innocence stirs an overpowering desire in Tony, but he senses that with this untouched beauty, he has to take it one slow, delicious step at a time. This is a romance to relish, a treat from Diane.

Linda Cajio begins **DANCING IN THE DARK,** LOVESWEPT #609, with an eye-opening scene in which the hero is engaged in a sacred ceremony and dancing naked in the woods! Jake Halford feels a little silly performing the men's movement ritual, but Charity Brown feels downright embarrassed at catching him at it. How can she ever work with her company's new vice president without remembering the thrilling sight of his muscles and power? The way Linda has these two learning how to mix business and pleasure is a pure delight.

HANNAH'S HUNK, LOVESWEPT #610 by Sandra Chastain, is nothing less than a sexy rebel with a southern drawl . . . and an ex-con whom Hannah Clendening "kidnaps" so he could pose for the cover of her Fantasy Romance. Dan Bailey agrees, but only if Hannah plays the heroine and he gets to kiss her. When desire flares between them like a force field, neither believes that what they feel could last. Of course Sandra, with her usual wit and charm, makes sure there's a happily ever after for this unusual couple.

Finally, there's **THE TROUBLE WITH MAGIC,** LOVESWEPT #611 by Mary Kay McComas. Harriet Wheaton has an outrageous plan to keep Payton Dunsmore from foreclosing on the great manor house on Jovette Island. Marooning them there, she tells him that she's trying to fulfill the old legend of enemies meeting on Jovette and falling in love! Payton's furious at first, but he soon succumbs to the enchantment of the island . . . and Harriet herself. Mary Kay delivers pure magic with this marvelous romance.

On sale this month from FANFARE are four outstanding novels. If you missed **TEMPERATURES RISING** by blockbuster author Sandra Brown when it first came out, now's your chance to grab a copy of this wonderfully evocative love story. Chantal duPont tells herself that she needs Scout Ritland only to build a much-needed bridge on the South Pacific island she calls home. And when the time comes for him to leave, she must make the painful decision of letting him go—or risking everything by taking a chance on love.

From beloved author Rosanne Bittner comes **OUTLAW HEARTS,** a stirring new novel of heart-stopping danger and burning desire. At twenty, Miranda Hayes has known more than her share of heartache and loss. Then she clashes with the notorious gunslinger Jake Harkner, a hard-hearted loner with a price on his head, and finds within herself a deep well of courage . . . and feelings of desire she's never known before.

Fanfare is proud to publish **THE LAST HIGHWAYMAN,** the first historical romance by Katherine O'Neal, a truly exciting new voice in women's fiction. In this delectable action-packed novel, Christina has money, power, and position, but she has never known reckless passion, never found enduring love . . . until she is kidnapped by a dangerously handsome bandit who needs her to heal his tormented soul.

In the bestselling tradition of Danielle Steel, **CONFI-DENCES** by Penny Hayden is a warm, deeply moving novel about four "thirty-something" mothers whose lives are interwoven by a long-held secret—a secret that could now save the life of a seventeen-year-old boy dying of leukemia.

Also available now in the hardcover edition from Double-day is **MASK OF NIGHT** by Lois Wolfe, a stunning historical novel of romantic suspense. When an actress and a cattle rancher join forces against a diabolical villain, the result is an unforgettable story of love and vengeance.

Happy reading!

With warmest wishes,

Nita Taublib

Nita Taublib
Associate Publisher
LOVESWEPT and FANFARE

OFFICIAL RULES TO WINNERS CLASSIC SWEEPSTAKES

No Purchase necessary. To enter the sweepstakes follow instructions found elsewhere in this offer. You can also enter the sweepstakes by hand printing your name, address, city, state and zip code on a 3" x 5" piece of paper and mailing it to: Winners Classic Sweepstakes, P.O. Box 785, Gibbstown, NJ 08027. Mail each entry separately. Sweepstakes begins 12/1/91. Entries must be received by 6/1/93. Some presentations of this sweepstakes may feature a deadline for the Early Bird prize. If the offer you receive does, then to be eligible for the Early Bird prize your entry must be received according to the Early Bird date specified. Not responsible for lost, late, damaged, misdirected, illegible or postage due mail. Mechanically reproduced entries are not eligible. All entries become property of the sponsor and will not be returned.

Prize Selection/Validations: Winners will be selected in random drawings on or about 7/30/93, by VENTURA ASSOCIATES, INC., an independent judging organization whose decisions are final. Odds of winning are determined by total number of entries received. Circulation of this sweepstakes is estimated not to exceed 200 million. Entrants need not be present to win. All prizes are guaranteed to be awarded and delivered to winners. Winners will be notified by mail and may be required to complete an affidavit of eligibility and release of liability which must be returned within 14 days of date of notification or alternate winners will be selected. Any guest of a trip winner will also be required to execute a release of liability. Any prize notification letter or any prize returned to a participating sponsor, Bantam Doubleday Dell Publishing Group, Inc., its participating divisions or subsidiaries, or VENTURA ASSOCIATES, INC. as undeliverable will be awarded to an alternate winner. Prizes are not transferable. No multiple prize winners except as may be necessary due to unavailability, in which case a prize of equal or greater value will be awarded. Prizes will be awarded approximately 90 days after the drawing. All taxes, automobile license and registration fees, if applicable, are the sole responsibility of the winners. Entry constitutes permission (except where prohibited) to use winners' names and likenesses for publicity purposes without further or other compensation.

Participation: This sweepstakes is open to residents of the United States and Canada, except for the province of Quebec. This sweepstakes is sponsored by Bantam Doubleday Dell Publishing Group, Inc. (BDD), 666 Fifth Avenue, New York, NY 10103. Versions of this sweepstakes with different graphics will be offered in conjunction with various solicitations or promotions by different subsidiaries and divisions of BDD. Employees and their families of BDD, its division, subsidiaries, advertising agencies, and VENTURA ASSOCIATES, INC., are not eligible.

Canadian residents, in order to win, must first correctly answer a time limited arithmetical skill testing question. Void in Quebec and wherever prohibited or restricted by law. Subject to all federal, state, local and provincial laws and regulations.

Prizes: The following values for prizes are determined by the manufacturers' suggested retail prices or by what these items are currently known to be selling for at the time this offer was published. Approximate retail values include handling and delivery of prizes. Estimated maximum retail value of prizes: 1 Grand Prize ($27,500 if merchandise or $25,000 Cash); 1 First Prize ($3,000); 5 Second Prizes ($400 each); 35 Third Prizes ($100 each); 1,000 Fourth Prizes ($9.00 each) ; 1 Early Bird Prize ($5,000); Total approximate maximum retail value is $50,000. Winners will have the option of selecting any prize offered at level won. Automobile winner must have a valid driver's license at the time the car is awarded. Trips are subject to space and departure availability. Certain black-out dates may apply. Travel must be completed within one year from the time the prize is awarded. Minors must be accompanied by an adult. Prizes won by minors will be awarded in the name of parent or legal guardian.

For a list of Major Prize Winners (available after 7/30/93): send a self-addressed, stamped envelope entirely separate from your entry to: Winners Classic Sweepstakes Winners, P.O. Box 825, Gibbstown, NJ 08027. Requests must be received by 6/1/93. DO NOT SEND ANY OTHER CORRESPONDENCE TO THIS P.O. BOX.

Women's Fiction

On Sale in February

TEMPERATURES RISING

56045-X $5.99/6.99 in Canada

☐ **by Sandra Brown**

New York Times bestselling author of
A WHOLE NEW LIGHT and FRENCH SILK
A contemporary tale of love and passion in the South Pacific.

OUTLAW HEARTS

29807-0 $5.99/6.99 in Canada

☐ **by Rosanne Bittner**

Bestselling author of SONG OF THE WOLF,
praised by *Romantic Times* as "a stunning
achievement...that moves the soul and fills the heart."

THE LAST HIGHWAYMAN

56065-4 $5.50/6.50 in Canada

☐ **by Katherine O'Neal**

Fascinating historical fact and sizzling romantic fiction meet
in this sensual tale of a legendary bandit and a scandalous
high-born lady.

CONFIDENCES

56170-7 $4.99/5.99 in Canada

☐ **by Penny Hayden**

"Thirtysomething" meets Danielle Steel—four best friends
are bound by an explosive secret.

Bestselling Women's Fiction

Sandra Brown

_____	29783-X A WHOLE NEW LIGHT	..... $5.99/6.99 in Canada
_____	29500-4 TEXAS! SAGE	.... $5.99/6.99
_____	29085-1 22 INDIGO PLACE	.... $4.50/5.50
_____	28990-X TEXAS! CHASE	.... $5.99/6.99
_____	28951-9 TEXAS! LUCKY	.... $5.99/6.99

Amanda Quick

_____	29316-8 RAVISHED	.... $4.99/5.99
_____	29315-X RECKLESS	.... $5.99/6.99
_____	29325-7 RENDEZVOUS	.... $4.99/5.99
_____	28932-2 SCANDAL	.... $4.95/5.95
_____	28354-5 SEDUCTION	.... $4.99/5.99
_____	28594-7 SURRENDER	.... $5.99/6.99

Nora Roberts

_____	29490-3 DIVINE EVIL	.... $5.99/6.99
_____	29597-7 CARNAL INNOCENCE	.... $5.50/6.50
_____	29078-9 GENUINE LIES	.... $4.99/5.99
_____	28578-5 PUBLIC SECRETS	.... $4.95/5.95
_____	26461-3 HOT ICE	.... $4.99/5.99
_____	26574-1 SACRED SINS	.... $5.50/6.50
_____	27859-2 SWEET REVENGE	.... $5.50/6.50
_____	27283-7 BRAZEN VIRTUE	.... $4.99/5.99

Iris Johansen

_____	29968-9 THE TIGER PRINCE	.... $5.50/6.50
_____	29871-2 LAST BRIDGE HOME	.... $4.50/5.50
_____	29604-3 THE GOLDEN BARBARIAN	.... $4.99/5.99
_____	29244-7 REAP THE WIND	.... $4.99/5.99
_____	29032-0 STORM WINDS	.... $4.99/5.99
_____	28855-5 THE WIND DANCER	.... $4.95/5.95

Ask for these titles at your bookstore or use this page to order.

Please send me the books I have checked above. I am enclosing $ _____ (add $2.50 to cover postage and handling). Send check or money order, no cash or C. O. D.'s please.

Mr./ Ms. _____

Address _____

City/ State/ Zip _____

Send order to: Bantam Books, Dept. FN 16, 2451 S. Wolf Road, Des Plaines, IL 60018

Please allow four to six weeks for delivery.

Prices and availability subject to change without notice.   FN 16 -3/93